CW00558295

About This

Remember those childhood stories about not walking on the cracks in the pavement? About mysterious bogeymen who would snatch naughty children, and the ghosts that dwelt in every abandoned or derelict building in the neighbourhood? Well, they grew up and they've returned.

Join 18 masters of the macabre, the strange, and the bizarre as they journey into a dark and richly reimagined Portsmouth that you will never forget. Here you can meet a man who finds himself transforming into the Tricorn Centre. Discover the mysterious pulse that beats beneath the pavement of this living city that craves blood and sacrifice. Witness damnation in a hellish vision of Victorian Portsmouth, and learn just how difficult it can be getting two severed heads through customs at the port. Like the waves that lap the fringes of this waterfront city, past and present flow back and forth in these tales of haunting and horror, dragging ghosts and their tragedies in their wake.

Bursting with historical, fantastical, crime, surreal and gothic fictions, this spine-tingling collection of short stories and poems will forever transform how you view Britain's only island city.

Books by Karl Bell

The Magical Imagination:
Magic and Modernity in Urban England 1780-1914

The Legend of Spring-heeled Jack:
Victorian Urban Folklore and Popular Cultures

Port Towns and Urban Cultures:
International Histories of the Waterfront, c.1700-2000
(with Brad Beaven and Robert James)

Books by Stephen Pryde-Jarman

The Resurrection of Thomas Zoot
Rubble Girl
John, Paul, George, Flamingo

Books from Life Is Amazing with a Portsmouth theme

Fiction
Portsmouth Fairy Tales for Grown-Ups
By Celia's Arbour (by Walter Besant and James Rice)
Day of the Dead (by members of Portsmouth Writers' Hub)

Non-Fiction
Conan Doyle and the Mysterious World of Light, 1887-1920
(by Matt Wingett)
Ten Years In A Portsmouth Slum (by Robert Dolling)
The History of Portsmouth (by Lake Allen)
Recollections of John Pounds (by Henry Hawkes)

edited by

Karl Bell

Stephen Pryde-Jarman

Life Is Amazing

A Life Is Amazing Paperback
Dark City
First published 2016 by Life Is Amazing
ISBN: 978-0-9956394-0-9
First Edition
Collection and Introduction © Karl Bell and Stephen Pryde-Jarman, 2016
Cover Photo © Catherine Taylor; Cover Design by Matt Wingett
All Rights Reserved.

Each author has asserted his or her right under the Copyright, Design and
Patent Act 1988 to be identified as the author of his or her work.

Concrete; Basements © Matt Parsons 2016
Clarendon Road, St Kitts, Gourlay, 1836 © Alison Habens 2016
The Ideas Man © Diana Bretherick 2016
The Boy with the Burberry Cap (Or Where the Traffic Lights Should Be); The
Spinnaker Tower © Rebecca Swarbrick 2016
Tide Will Tell © V H Leslie 2016
Undercurrent © Justin MacCormack 2016
Cracked City © James Bicheno 2016
Imprints on the Air © Helen Salsbury 2016
Two Heads ©William Sutton 2016
Killing Time © Jacqui Pack 2016
Still Dark Water © Nick Morrish 2016
Restless © Andrew Bailey2016
The Rhythm © Charlotte Comley 2016
On the Wharves © Tom Millman 2016
Tartarus© Joseph Matthew Pierce 2016
See How They Run © Susan Shipp 2016
Waiting at the End of the Line © Sue Evans 2016
Fragmented Self - Roz Ryszka-Onions

Please contact the individual writers directly if you would like to discuss
reproducing, quoting or any other aspect of their work.

Please note, this book is entirely a work of fiction. The names, characters and
incidents portrayed in it are the work of the authors' imaginations. Any
resemblance to actual persons, living or dead, or events is entirely
coincidental.

Dedication:

To our families, constant lights in any dark city:
(Karl) Jo, Luca and Evan, and
(Stephen) Laura, Annabelle and Rosie.

Acknowledgements:

The editors would like to thank the fabulous writers of Portsmouth for their wonderful creativity, hard work, and professionalism. They would also like to acknowledge the energy and enthusiasm of the Portsmouth Writers' Hub in supporting this project. They would especially like to thank Tessa Ditner, William Sutton, Diana Bretherick and Matt Wingett for all their help, support and encouragement. Without this special combination of people and local talent this book would never have happened. Karl would also like to thank the University of Portsmouth's Faculty of Humanities and Social Science and CEISR for financing the 'Supernatural Cities' project, from which the initial idea for a story collection grew. Finally we would like to thank Portsmouth, that sometimes grubby, sometimes grizzled, but endlessly charming old dame of the sea front. Her streets, buildings, histories and people have been the inspiration for all the stories gathered here.

Contents

A Friendly Note of Warning

There is a city that exists in the corner of your eye. You have always known this. You have felt it there, just out of sight, just out of reach. On occasion you may have even glimpsed it, although you may immediately regret having done so. But should you turn to look at it directly you know it will slip from view as surely as a ghost.

This city looks a lot like Portsmouth but the Portsmouth that peeks from behind the walls, that hides behind masks woven from the mundane. Its bricks are made of memory and loss, imagination and dark emotion, especially longing and dread, and there is more than a little blood and magic in its old mortar. The scenery may be familiar, like a half-remembered dream, but be warned, its inhabitants are likely to be ghosts or murderers or madmen. The supernatural has always gathered at boundaries, at margins, and what is Portsmouth, this waterfront city, but a dwelling place built upon that most important boundary between sea and land. It has long been a port, a gateway, a place of exchange; a city built of stories about comings and goings, disappearances and returns.

You cannot map this elusive city. It arrives with dusk and departs with dawn, and puts everything back the way it was after its midnight play. Well, almost. Yet here, through this collection of stories and the brave writers who penned them, we have assembled some intrepid guides. When, on a suitably dark and blustery January evening, I challenged local writers to respond to the theme of the dark city I could never have imagined that they would conjure such rich tales. These stories may frequently evoke the supernatural and macabre but they are, at the same time, grounded in being human, alive with a sense of what it means to be a city dweller.

Interestingly, many are written from a first person perspective, thereby reinforcing a sense that we experience cities subjectively, from behind the walls of ourselves, each looking out from the rooms of our own mind upon subtly different versions of the same landscape. Urban living is often a phantasmal experience. We daily pass ghostlike strangers and there are ghosts aplenty in these tales. Ghosts of the past and present, of dark deeds and dismal lives. Ghosts of our own making, occasionally even of ourselves or the lives we have left behind.

Some of these encounters with the dark city are rooted in the familiarity of Portsmouth landmarks, points by which we evolved urbanites have learnt to navigate our way around. Others, like the Tricorn, are now a ghostly architecture, a lingering memory that casts an indelible shadow upon those rebuilt spaces. Beyond hauntings, some of these stories allude to more visionary horrors, articulating our sense that there is always more to the city (and perhaps ourselves) than we can ever see or know; concealed, waiting, and quite possibly hungry.

These stories take us through a murky netherworld, a dark reflection of the city we know. As many of the world's mythologies teach us, there is always a price for trespassing through the underworld and this book is no exception. The price is simply this; be prepared to never see parts of Portsmouth in the same way again.

If you are willing to pay such a price then by all means come in, walk through the darkened streets of this city that exists at the boundaries between reality and imagination. Just be aware that they might be occupied by spectres or speckled with blood. Hold your guide's hand tightly or else risk becoming lost in this other Portsmouth's creeping, entangling darkness. Tread carefully. And watch for those cracks in the pavement.

You can't say you weren't warned.

Karl Bell and Stephen Pryde-Jarman,
Portsmouth, September 2016

Dark City

Concrete

Matt Parsons

'What would you say if I told you I thought I was turning into the Tricorn Centre?' asked Kieran.

Tony took another sip of his beer and looked through the window while he considered the question. It was getting dark outside. A huge, futuristic-looking yacht covered in lights was moored near the Spinnaker Tower.

'I think I'd probably say... maybe you are turning into the Tricorn. Maybe both of us are. I mean, I'm out of shape and going a bit grey, so there are obvious similarities. Hopefully we won't get demolished any time soon though.'

Kieran nodded.

Tony and Kieran had been friends since school. Tony lived in a modern tower block in Gunwharf known as The Lipstick. Kieran lived ten minutes away, in a Victorian semi-detached house, just off Elm Grove. They rarely had time to see each other. Kids, work, partners and countless other things got in the way. And then, one day, Kieran called and suggested they meet for a quiet drink in a bar in Gunwharf. But the bar wasn't quiet. Even though it was a dismal Wednesday evening in late September, the place was crowded.

'So... what's all this about, then?' asked Tony.

'I'm not sure,' said Kieran, as he picked at the edge of a beer mat. 'Seriously, though... if I said I was turning into the Tricorn, what would you say?'

'I don't know. I don't really understand what you're getting at.'

Kieran nodded. 'That's more or less what I said to her,' he muttered.

'Who?' said Tony

'Joanna,' said Kieran.

'Joanna thinks she's turning into the Tricorn?' Tony put his pint down. It wasn't easy to imagine Kieran's wife being put to use as a shopping centre and car park.

'She thought she was, yes,' said Kieran, 'for a couple of days last month.'

Tony leaned closer, straining to hear over the chatter, the laughter, and the muffled thump of the music in the background.

'I know it sounds unbelievable,' said Kieran. 'But it's true.' He rubbed his forehead. 'She won't talk about it now. She'd kill me if she knew I'd told anyone.'

The smirk faded from Tony's lips. He'd been waiting for the punch-line. Now he was beginning to worry that Kieran wasn't joking.

'She said she'd been hallucinating that she'd become the Tricorn Centre,' said Kieran. 'Can you imagine what it's like to hear your wife tell you she thinks she weighs thousands of tonnes and is made entirely of concrete?'

Tony looked down at the disappearing froth on his beer. 'Ah,' he said. He twisted the glass round.

'The doctors checked her over, but they couldn't find anything wrong with her,' said Kieran. 'It's ok, she's fine now. It's like it never happened. But at the time, she was really disturbed by it. So was I. Oh, and before you ask, she hadn't been drinking, there were no drugs involved, she didn't have a temperature, and she wasn't delirious. There's no explanation for it.' He reached into his rucksack. 'No explanation, that is, apart from this.' Kieran emptied the carrier bag onto the table. A lump of concrete roughly the size of a brick landed with a clunk. 'A genuine piece of Tricorn concrete,' said Kieran. 'This is the cause of it, according to Joanna.'

Tony stared at it. 'That's not really a piece of the Tricorn though, is it?'

Kieran scratched his beard. 'I don't know,' he said. 'Maybe it is, maybe it isn't. It cost me fifteen quid though, from a shop on Albert Road. Yeah, I know, they must have seen me coming. It was one of her birthday presents. She's always saying they should have kept the Tricorn, so I thought she'd find it funny. Anyway, she didn't. She said it was creepy for some reason, told me to throw it away. Then, of course, she had these funny turns... but once I'd hidden the thing in the garage, she got better.'

'Why didn't you just get rid of it?'

'I don't know,' said Kieran. 'I thought maybe you might want it as a souvenir, seeing as you worked there and everything. I suppose it's just my miserly streak. I couldn't bring myself to chuck it away. It'd be like chucking away fifteen quid, wouldn't it?'

Tony picked up the piece of concrete. It was surprisingly heavy. One side of it was smooth and felt almost oily to the touch. The other surfaces were jagged and dusty. There was a gold foil sticker attached which read: GENUINE TRICORN CONCRETE. Tony looked at Kieran. Kieran was watching him closely.

'Feel anything?' said Kieran.

'No,' said Tony. 'Should I?'

'Probably not,' said Kieran.

Tony closed his front door. He switched on the light, kicked off his shoes, and slung the piece of concrete onto the sofa. There were dirty cups and plates in the sink, newspapers on the floor, and the remains of an overcooked microwave lasagne on the table next to a filthy pair of oven gloves. The light on the answer phone was blinking. It wouldn't be a message from Amy. They'd been separated for a couple of months, and hadn't spoken for over two weeks. When Kieran had asked him how Amy was, Tony heard himself say: 'Oh, she's fine,' and then quickly change the subject. It wasn't just embarrassment. Tony knew that Amy and Kieran had never got on. Amy would often make snide remarks about Kieran, and they'd never seemed comfortable in each other's company. Somehow, it would have seemed disloyal to talk to Kieran about Amy. Tony's finger hovered over the answer phone play button for an instant.

Maybe he should delete the message without listening to it; it was bound to be an automated call. Most of his answer phone messages were automated calls. He pressed the play button anyway.

'You were called today at eight-seventeen...' the robotic voice droned.

'Get on with it,' Tony snapped. There was a click, and the recorded message played back.

'Our records indicate you may have been involved in an accident...'

Tony swore and jabbed his finger on the delete button.

'Message deleted.'

He slumped back onto the sofa. So that was it, then. Another day done.

Tony didn't sleep well. He woke up early, but lay in bed until nine o'clock. Then he got up, pulled on his jog pants and an old t-shirt, and stood on the balcony drinking tea. On the pavement below, the crowds were congregating: little kids screaming and pulling on their mother's arms, shoppers struggling with bags and texting as they walked, and teenagers leaning over the railings, smoking.

The old Georgian Naval building was now a pub, and the figurehead of HMS Vernon kept watch over a gallery and delicatessen. It was as if the remnants of Portsmouth's history were being crowded out by shiny glass fronted restaurant chains and fashion outlet stores.

Tony finished his tea, closed the windows and sat on the sofa. On the wall above the television was a framed map of Portsmouth and Southsea dating from the 1930s. He'd bought it from the gallery in Gunwharf, and he'd spent more time looking at the map than watching television. He could point out the narrow terraced house in North End where his grandparents had lived. He'd located the spot where his childhood home would be built. But the part of the map which fascinated Tony the most was the area around Charlotte Street. It was an unrecognisable chaos of twisting alleyways, crammed with buildings of every shape, which had been demolished to make way for the Tricorn Shopping Centre. The Tricorn was where Tony spent much of his youth: shopping with his mum when he was a little kid, working in Charlotte Street Superstore on Saturdays, and hanging around on a BMX bike when there was nothing else to do on a Sunday. Now the Tricorn was history, too: demolished to make way for a car park. But Tony took comfort in the idea that history could leave a mark on a place: that somehow the past could live on, and that the stories of the city could be absorbed into the brickwork, tarmac and concrete. Absorbed into pieces of concrete like the one lying next to him, forgotten, on the sofa.

As he touched it, he felt a stinging jolt of electricity. He snatched his hand away. Surprised, he hesitated for a moment, and then cautiously tapped it with the tip of his finger. There was no shock this time. He picked up the concrete and sniffed it. There was a faint mineral tang, and subtle notes of car exhausts, rubbish bins, and Chinese food. He stroked the smooth surface. The sticker bothered him, so he peeled it off and flicked it across the room. He lay back on the sofa with the concrete weighing heavily on his chest, listening to the ticking of the clock. He really should get up, switch on the laptop and start work. He closed his eyes. The smell of the concrete lingered. It should have been unpleasant, but he felt comforted by it. He could picture the tarmac beneath his feet, spotted with trodden down chewing gum, and hear the sounds of Charlotte Street Market: 'Come on, get your pears, 30p a pound ...' The rumbling of cars resonated within him, and spiralled through him. He was a vast labyrinth, ringing with the echoes of footsteps. The breeze whipped through him, bringing with it the smell of bins. His consciousness swept up steps and down fire escapes, around curved concrete, across filthy sheets of glass, to a large space filled with shoppers. He saw every angle of Charlotte Street Superstore at once; a cubist chaos of market stalls in a huge space, lit by fluorescent tubes. There were rows of stalls, with racks of leather jackets, stacks of plates and piles of fabric. He followed a staircase up to the balcony, to a second hand clothes shop, record store and cafe. Sitting at a table, reading a copy of the NME, was a young woman. It was Amy.

Amy was young. She was wearing a batwing fluffy pink jumper, clear lip gloss and blue mascara. She flicked her permed hair away from her eyes, and then took a drag of her cigarette. She looked up and smiled. A young man was standing at her side. She stood up and wrapped her arms around him, and they kissed for some time. Tony was spying on his own future wife. He knew he should turn away, but he couldn't. The couple drew apart, and Amy smiled... and then Tony realised. The young man was Kieran. Now, it was clear why Amy and Kieran had never seemed to get on with each other. They had a history. A history they'd kept secret. Tony was stunned. It felt like a wrecking ball had slammed into him. He gasped and opened his eyes.

The sensation of hot blood in his veins was startling. His skin tingled, his hair stood up on the back of his neck, and his heart thudded in his chest. What had just happened? Only a second ago, Tony had been made of concrete, occupying an area of over one hundred and seventy-four thousand square feet, able to support the weight of four hundred and fifty cars, with sufficient space for fifty-five shops, two pubs and a supermarket. He had, for one brief moment, become the Tricorn.

Tony sat up. The concrete rolled off his chest and landed on the rug with a thud. He jumped up and stepped away from it, wiping his hands on his jog pants.

He picked up his mobile phone with shaking hands and called Kieran, but the call went straight to his answer phone. Tony hung up. The room was spinning. He wanted that piece of concrete out of his flat, but he couldn't risk touching it. He glanced over at the oven gloves on the table. Maybe they'd be enough to protect him. He needed to think ... but first he needed to calm down.

Tony stumbled to the newsagents, bought a packet of cigarettes and a lighter for the first time in over ten years, and returned home. He stood on the balcony and lit a cigarette. It tasted horrible. He felt his phone vibrate in his pocket. It was Kieran.

Tony held the vibrating phone in his hand. Amy and Kieran had gone out with each other. He'd seen the evidence. But why had they kept it from him? Tony rejected the call and put the phone back in his pocket. He put out his cigarette. He felt lightheaded. He could see things more clearly now. He threw the remaining cigarettes in the bin, closed the curtains, and sat on the sofa. The room was dark. He had to know more. And there was only one way it was likely to happen.

His pulse raced. He took a deep breath. He grabbed the concrete and closed his eyes. Instantly his body was massive, cold and immobile. He felt the rumbling of tyres, felt the weight pressing on every pillar. He felt the tread of feet on his stairs. He felt seagulls jab him with their sharp beaks as they pecked at a half-eaten hamburger, and felt their webbed feet patter over him as they squabbled.

Tony had become every part of the Tricorn, from the tarmac surface of the highest level of the car park to the deepest layer of the hardcore in the foundations. He had become every stairwell, every fluorescent strip light, every plastic sign, and every inch of graffitied concrete. The sun rose and beat down on him, frost formed on him, dark stains spread over his walls. Rain dripped through fissures in his vast body, forming stalactites.

The sun and the moon wheeled overhead with dizzying speed. Tony struggled to regain control, focusing on one small part of himself: a flickering strip light on a ceiling somewhere in his upper interior. The passage of sun and moon slowed, and his panic subsided. Some distant part of him vibrated with the stamping of feet and the throbbing of speaker cabinets. He felt the tiniest of scratches, more of a tickling sensation, and turned his attention towards it. Somehow he already knew what he what he was going to see. A younger Tony was scratching his initials into the concrete wall of a stairwell with a penknife. It was his last day of work. His legs were skinny, and his hair was scraped back into a pony tail. He was wearing black jeans with holes at the knee, a baggy camouflage t-shirt and orange baseball boots. Tony watched his younger self take one last look around, and then walk down the stairs, until only the echoes of his footsteps remained.

His attention snapped back to the rumbling and thudding above. There was a nightclub up there. His consciousness surged through concrete and wire, through metal and plastic, through a double doorway, into a sticky floored drinking hole. Amy was there. She was standing at the bar talking some friends. The music was loud, and Amy was leaning over and shouting into another girl's ear. Kieran was sitting at a table on the other side of the dance floor, his eyes shining in the flashing lights, his hair plastered to his face.

And then Kieran left with someone else. He passed Amy without a glance. Tony felt himself growing cold, contracting, and creaking. The fissures which had opened up in his body were deeper. It began to rain, and the sun rose. Men in visibility jackets and hard hats wandered around. Kids pulled wheelies on BMXs and fences went up. The Charlotte Street Superstore was empty. The Chinese Restaurant was empty. Tony felt pigeons scratching him. The sun rose countless times. And then the bulldozers arrived.

Tony tried to open his eyes, but he couldn't. He didn't have eyes. He tried to move, but he had no legs and no arms. He wanted to scream, but he had no mouth. He heard and felt the rumbling of caterpillar tracks. He knew that slowly, very slowly over the course of several weeks, he was going to be destroyed. He tried to stay calm. He needed to imagine himself in the future, sitting on the sofa in his flat with a piece of concrete in his hands. From somewhere very distant came the sound of a telephone, a click, and a droning voice.

'Our records indicate you may have been involved in an accident ...'

Tony gulped down a lungful of air. He was sitting on the sofa. The answer phone was recording another automated PPI call. He'd been the Tricorn Shopping Centre for what had seemed like months, but less than half an hour had passed. The piece of concrete was lying on the floor. He knew what he had to do. Minutes later, Tony was running through Gunwharf in his jog pants and dirty t-shirt. He was unshaven, his hair was sticking up, and he was holding a piece of concrete at arm's length in his oven-gloved hands. Crowds parted as

maps? You may see one twice if they're traveling quicker than the car or take a short cut. But they never actually move.

Mermaid, is it? At first I think, no legs: a princess with a seaweed sash. Bedraggled ringlets, pinned by a limpet crown. She is looking up at one of the houses; swiping right, I follow her gaze. Salt-crusted stucco, some fine gent's frontage, back in the Georges' day. Her face is blurred, that's normal for somebody caught unknowing by the googles. But this: as I back away, and the street view shifts, her blurry face turns to look at me. I back up Clarendon Road, clicking wildly, and I'm sure she watches me go.

When I get home... Wait, I was already home. Panting but I never left the house. Safe but shattered: I did see it, real as anything, on the screen. I feel like I've been out and need to go to bed though it is still only three in the morning. Hours till dawn: I lie there shaking, real as anything, under the sheets.

When I dream, it's like the internet again. Everybody in the world shouting in capitals, swearing in ****s; sharing every meme I can imagine, and many I can't believe. What plastic button will it take to reboot me? Twelve hours, half the sun's day, and I'm still riding behind the grim-veiled windows of the street view car.

Then cereal, no milk. Even the coke has run dry today. There is always water; stone cold, pipe fresh, flowing freely from the tap. Always water to drink, here, and a safe, comfortable place to pee; which is why I stay indoors. I've street viewed the public loos on Southsea seafront but, to me, they are as convenient as squatting in a rolling hold aswim with shit, in front of my vomiting compatriots.

When I get very hungry I go to look at the Premier, a corner shop, on street view. There is always the same customer coming out with a bar of chocolate. Obviously, I can't go inside. When I am nearly dying I get out of the warm flat and actually walk by the leafy back lanes to the store, and really go in. But that's not this day. Still got loads of molasses in the fridge. And sometimes I don't even eat it, just open the door and look into the light.

After breakfast I boot up and swashbuckle with a brick-built Johnny Depp as his Lego figurehead, beached on the rocky Lego

Caribbean. Six weeks, hiding under the covers, sweating rum. Then I go down the road at dusk, in my pyjamas. Street view says it's May, about 2pm and cloudy. Not many people about; zip-up jumper man, a woman crossing the threshold. Patrolling on my own portal, I know exactly who is supposed to be walking there, and who is not.

My eyes: I think there's something wrong with my eyes. I know who should be frozen mid-stride, and who I should not see. Street view is playing tricks on me. God, it's the girl I saw first on the prom where she wasn't before. Then I saw her on the other side of the road. My eyes are spilling sea down my face, I am so afraid. That girl has moved again.

She is half way up Clarendon Road, at the junction with Waverly and Granada; by the wall where the city's own Banksy has immortalised it. On a house end, bombed off abruptly in World War II, a mural: Pompey as a minor promontory, laced with major roads in bright yellow, customised with a life-sized cast from its colourful cultural history.

That is not there anymore: the brilliant blue sea still outlines it but the island has changed shape; no longer squat, a dash and a dot, a whalebone in the water. The girl is walking straight past this painted wall, minutes from my home, and the landmark mural has changed beyond recognition. There are place-names written on the map but when I zoom in they're unreadable, though I take screen shots and enlarge them to the limit.

She strides by in a long mussel-shell-black skirt that clings glistening to her legs; a blouse frilly as sea-spume and a bonnet that seems to be trimmed with bladder-wrack. She is coming my way. I do not go on-line again for the rest of the day.

In the middle of the night, life is the internet, though; and when I search for the landmass, tilted like a bottle of yo-ho-ho, I get great results. It's St Kitt's; an emerald set in the Caribbean. Suddenly, on a Southsea wall, the likeness of a West Indian island is painted. Is that weird? Would anyone else even notice this glitch on their overcast screen?

In the morning; no cereal, no milk. Only the water is running today. There is always water, sea everywhere, warm and salty; and rum flowing freely from the tap. When I get very hungry I go to look at the shop on street view. There is always the same customer coming out with a bar of chocolate. When I am nearly dying I walk by the leafy back lanes to the corner shop and actually go in. That is the next day. Only got a little molasses in the fridge, spilt on the bottom shelf in a dark brown shape like tea leaves foretelling the sinking of a clipper.

At dusk, I go to Google, to view the street again, to check whether time has stood still in Southsea, May 2015. Or whether a ship-fucked figurehead has come out of the Solent and is striding up the road towards me, dripping barnacles and brine.

She has passed the corner shop. I can see the storefront behind her. Gourlay's. Wait. That's not its name. It's normally called Premier; I've seen it a hundred times before. I've seen the white on a purple background, yellow dot over the I, cursive letters about a foot tall, spelling it out with the P to the r to the e; but now it definitely says G. Gourlay's. I keep refreshing the screen.

Possibly I pass out. When my page is reloaded, I'm back in the barrel, trying to breathe Lego bubbles. Water's grimy as the Solent, not the West Indian sea; and I'm crying for the pirate captain, under the covers. I tire myself out sobbing and, in the end, the smell of my own rum sweat makes me swoon.

When I dream, it's like the game again. Everybody shouting in capitals, swearing in ****s; sharing every meme I can imagine, and many I can't believe. What whalebone button will it take to reboot me?

Twelve hours, half the sun's sail, and I'm still riding behind the grimy portholes of the Lego galleon. Ship's out of rations: no cereal, no milk. I have to go out of the house. No rum. The real me, not pixelated, not plastic bricked; I leave through the actual front door, painted. The world is too sudden after my long sea voyage. I surge up the street, running aground on the 3D kerb. Though I keep a constant look out over my shoulder, I see no girls in surf-frilled blouses coming to google me back.

It's hard to walk through the shop door; can't pass this portal in street view, so it feels wrong now. I try to keep my mind a complete blank while inside; don't want to lose lives where there's no chance to buy life back. The sun is out when I emerge from the dark cave of the corner store and I suddenly remember where energy really comes from, when it's not that dull old spring day on the internet.

It comes from the moment: flesh and blood reactions, the photosynthesis, the physics. Walking in the air, breathing its saltiness; I recall the appeal of real life. I can't stay in that place for long, because it is possible for somewhere to be too real, too raw, too unreliable. I need to transition back to my house as quick as a flash, so dizzy by the time I'm at the front door, I hardly know whether it's digital (or a[na]log[ue]). But as soon as I'm in my stale bed, belly full of fresh sugar rations, laptop open, I go rushing out again into the virtual neighbourhood.

Wind in my sails I click on the map, losing my bearings in a windy backstreet, then scrolling out on to Clarendon Road again. In the familiar grey light, a bus shelter; striding past it, the girl, with bonnet ribbons like fronds of seaweed flowing over her shoulders as she walks. And behind her, on the bus-stop, these numbers where the timetable usually is: 1836.

She is no street view person; she is some siren or shaman, a spirit who can shift between levels, superimpose on the wrong scene, a glitch in the game. And I'm quite the player, I would take her on, I could tackle her; if she comes any closer than the bus stop at the 'circle'. It's one of those with a full-length hording, and advertising images which scroll round with a rattling sound, so when I click back to it the picture has changed: no longer the big date but a life-size image of the scene I saw told in brown sugar (spilled in my fridge): a shipwreck made of shit.

And now it's not just pictures but I seem to hear a voice, too, her voice, though I haven't got headphones on:

I was so sick on the voyage home, nobody would have believed me a naval captain's daughter. Poisoned nearly to death by the swollen Atlantic, I started to believe my companions were turning into the cargo. Mrs Shore, rolling like a barrel of rum loosed in the hold, distilling amber stains on silk-stretched bosom and belly. Oh, and the stench of her fermented incontinence.

The two Miss Shores were turning to sugar. Pale, sticky round the lips, still refined as they kissed me in our misery. The littler children were melting like molasses, brown-limbed babies grown in the Empire's hottest sun, now oozing like jars of treacle on their long sail back to England.

I don't just play games. I know how to be serious on the internet, too. All the wisdom of the wide world is found with six well-chosen key words; and within a few clicks, I have the identity of the girl, my on-line stalker. 'Clarendon Road, St Kitt's, Gourlay, 1836'.

But then I carry on playing games. They're addictive, like stalking. And a girl can get serious in Lego, too. That session, I hear her answers through the speakers. A voice from long ago but not so very far away:

There was land. After six weeks at sea, there was land. And the land was going to kill us, if the sea hadn't. I could see the rocky outline of salvation, I could see the jagged cliffs, at the very Southern-most reach of the Isle of Wight. Nearly home, to the safe shingle beach and the common green grass and the grey spring days in Southsea. But getting through that portal would be impossible.

There were lights. I could see men on the rocky shoreline, small as Lego figures. Lanterns held aloft, fishermen's hats, burly and bearded, they were trying hard to save us. One tied himself to a rope and waded into the white water, where stone swords were ready to sever him from it.

Over the roar of water, the smash of ship's timber; over the screaming of children, the crash of falling mast. Under the water, the hiss of silence, the ear-pounding of my own blood, the lung-punching. Under the sea, in that plastic transparency, I was drifting slowly away; but I had so nearly made it, home to Portsmouth, to the foot of my father's garden, to Captain Gourlay's seafront villa...

1836 is already a vintage season. They erected the lighthouse at Chale, that year, to save other ships from the Clarendon's fate. It shocked the whole nation, with sad accounts of the poor little Miss Shores washed up all torn and tattered. And the dress I died in was already outdated; made for the start not the end of my trip to the colonies, it was worn out and out of fashion. But it was still on my body, when they found it. (Not ashore with the others, my travelling companions, at St Catherine's cruel point, but washed up gently on the sloping pebbles of Southsea.)

That's my cereal, my milk, today. That's my rum and coke. My dark chocolate sea-sickness. I'm out of food in my warm flat, again; and I think I might have pissed on the floor. The on-line version of my street is way scarier than actually going out, now. And if I go out, won't she come in?

I resist the temptation to shop at Gourlay's for one or two days more; it's hard to tell the time when the floor rocks to and fro like a famous shipwreck. I don't want to keep going over and over it. The only time I get outside is in street view. Every evening, I walk around in Google Maps. Clicking along the garden terraces, scrolling up the Thomas Owen facades, skirting the common to the seafront. It is still one day in May 2015; the grey spring afternoon when the streets where I live were captured.

That virtual walk round the block keeps me fit. Not my legs, which are Mermaid-like. Not my mind, which is fucked like a shipwrecked figurehead. Not my arms, they barely move though my bust heaves-ho. But it exercises my fingers as it enraptures my eyes.

The next time, and the last time, I look at my house in street view she is outside. She's leaning to look in through my grey net curtains. She is right outside my house. I know it is just the internet, just the screen, just the game, just a dream; I know it's not real, not here and not now. But: I look up, at my window. Because: dull afternoon, with that same cloudy light captured in May 2015.

All the vintage seasons are happening here, all the dark stories of Southsea unfolding now. I look up, at my window. My eyes: there's something wrong with... There is a head. Her shape, made monstrous by a bonnet; the exact outline from street view but seen from the other side. When I googled her, I was astounded by that mermaid's tale. Now Sarah Gourlay has found me.

But it wasn't me she was looking for. It was her brick-built father, with a house on South Parade. This is the story, told on a backwater website: while the bodies of the other women and girls belonging to another Captain were smashed ashore at the Isle of Wight and wept over by smugglers in their cove, Sarah Gourlay's body was not recovered. Until it was washed up at her family home, at Southsea (http://backofthewight.co.uk/clarendon.htm).

She swam, in death; around the white cliffs of the Island, through the grimy shallows of the Solent. Lifeless figurehead, broken mermaid; her heart steered home long after it stopped beating in the salty water. Love in fluid has made more incredible journeys before but still, I'm no swimmer and I so admire her spunk.

Barely able to walk, I make it eventually to the window. I sweep aside the curtain to see the brave face, under a barnacled bonnet. Victorious girl, with a seaweed sash; but beyond the gauzy drape, a gruesome blur... There's something wrong with my eyes. Sarah, not as she was at the start of her trip to the colonies; young, pretty, alive. But Miss Gourlay as she would have looked to whoever found her on the beach after a week in the water and a bit of a bashing at Blackgang Chine before that.

She's blind, bloated, peeling, purple in places; fish have eaten her cheeks. I stare bravely at the drowned face for ages: long enough to let me level up. So I'm not just a Lego piece in the game; but a proper pawn, able to make moves. I go boldly out of doors to help Sarah Gourlay find her father, the naval captain, after she troubled herself to get home dead.

When I first street viewed her, she was looking up at one of the houses with salt-crusted stucco. I walk down to the seafront to help her find it. The real me, not pixelated, not plastic bricked; though I am shitting myself. Like being shipwrecked all over again; I surge up the street, running aground on the kerb. Her skirt waves with every step, a long splash of surf breaking on the pavement.

Walking in real life past the regency crescent, I look up and see the portal. Playing on a Nintendo DS, on the rusty balcony; the youth from May 2015 slightly older now, longer haired. My street view soulmate. Our eyes actually meet. He stops playing the game and holds my gaze for the length of his terrace. I don't really know what I look like any more, but the way he looks at me, I could well be wearing a long mussel-shell-black dress and bladder-wrack-beribboned bonnet, a favourite character from a vintage season.

When I get to the sea... Wait, I was already at the sea. Panting but I never left the beach. I lie down where I think Sarah Gourlay's body was washed up. I'm probably miles out, as the internet doesn't say which exact spot the Captain's house stood on; but the end of Clarendon Road, to a Street View geek, a Google Map nerd, must be a working hypothesis.

Six weeks lying on the Southsea shingle till my very bones have become the stones. There are lights, strung along the shoreline like the little Miss Shore's necklaces, pearl-shine for their souls. I don't really know what I look like any more. But out of the corner of my eye, I can see the net-veiled windows of my father's house. Six weeks dying and I still feel tired. What pearly button will it take to reboot me?

The Ideas Man

Diana Bretherick

I didn't use to believe in monsters, except perhaps the human kind. Now I know differently. You see, now I know they exist but the problem is, no one believes me or if they do they're just not telling.

As a criminologist I'd come across plenty of human monsters. Most people are at least capable of committing evil acts and a small but significant number actually do. My research focused on the experience of committing violent crime. I wanted to find out how it felt so I decided that I would record evil in an effort to capture its essence. In doing so I hoped the name Dr Harry Price would become legendary in criminology. I imagined playing a starring role at conferences and perhaps there would even be a television series. I saw myself striding along dark passages in various European cities in a pair of sharp chinos, earnestly describing my take on some killer's dark deeds and explaining my brilliant theories to the enthralled viewer.

My research methods were unorthodox. Essentially, via classified ads in various publications, I invited anyone who had committed a violent crime to contact me and tell me about it. Complete confidentiality was assured. Whatever they told me, I would keep their identity to myself. Ethically it broke every rule in the book but by then I was so intoxicated by my idea I simply ignored the guidelines, thinking I knew better. As a result of a conversation with a colleague I had created a contraption to assist in my work. I won't bore you with the details except to say it was a special kind of recording instrument that took people's accounts and measured their reactions, leaving me with a distillation of their emotions. It was based on a machine used in the nineteenth century, by the world's first criminologist – an Italian called Lombroso. I had found a blueprint in some of his papers on display at a museum in Turin in the university where he was a Professor. He had found some material dating back to the sixteenth century in an archive and used it for his own work. All I had to do was apply a little science and adapt it for my needs. The machine I created was portable, if a little unwieldy but I had found an old leather Gladstone bag that fitted the machine both practically and aesthetically.

My office at the University was in a large and draughty Victorian building called Ravelin House, which had an interesting and turbulent history. In the nineteenth century it housed senior army officers when the park that now surrounds it was the city's garrison headquarters. Later Ravelin was Lord Montgomery's home during the Second World War. He was supposed to haunt the place after his wife died there but I'd never encountered him or any other ghosts for that matter. One evening I thought I had, but it turned out to be one of my colleagues who came in to work so infrequently that I didn't recognise him.

It was November and the evening was a stormy one. The trees in Ravelin Park creaked ominously with every gust, as if any moment they might come crashing down onto the few hardy students who were valiantly pushing their way against the wind towards the university library. It was already late. I conducted my office interviews after hours. This was partly to ensure anonymity for my subjects but there was also a tinge of academic caution. I had convinced myself I was a pioneer and was terrified that someone else would get wind of it and publish first. The exception was my colleague Dr Jim Pascoe, a historian who was so caught up in his own research that he had little interest in anyone else's. He occupied the room above mine and also worked late, sometimes staying long into the night. I told him I was conducting interviews without going into detail and he agreed to listen out for anything unusual. It was Jim that started it all, when he told me about his work on alchemy and the origins of scientific experimentation. He didn't know about his influence, which, I felt, leant the scheme a certain pleasing symmetry.

The doorbell rang. I remember feeling a shiver of anticipation travel down my spine as I went down the stairs to answer it. This was to be my final subject and I had saved the best till last. That night though there was something else – an added prickle of fear as I saw his bulky shadow through the glass. When I opened the door the man seized my hand and clasped it so hard I thought the bones in my fingers would crack. For someone in his late fifties he was clearly extremely fit.

'Dr Price, what a delight to meet you!' he boomed through his abundant beard as I ushered him in.

'Mr Hohenheim, thanks for coming out on such a wet night. It's really good of you.'

'Well I wouldn't say 'good', would you?

I laughed nervously as I showed him the way. He was so close behind me as he followed me up the stairs that I could smell his breath – peppermints and whisky.

Obviously I was taking a risk. But I knew that potentially he offered something special to my project. His letter had made that clear. Philip Hohenheim claimed to have been party to evil of such magnitude that, he wrote, it was entirely possible I would not believe him. Under normal circumstances that would have been enough to reject him as a subject but there was something about the way he described what he offered that made his inclusion irresistible. My other subjects, though useful, had been humdrum in comparison. A reformed wife beater (or so he claimed), a couple of burglars and a bank robber as well as some more serious violent offenders from local prisons had all described their experiences but I was unconvinced that evil at the level I was seeking could be found in any of them. I was about to abandon the present study, perhaps writing it up as a pilot when Philip Hohenheim contacted me.

Once he was hooked up to my recording equipment he told me his story. It made the accounts of others in his murderous trade seem positively amateur. Essentially he had been slaughtering his way around Europe with an enthusiasm and dedication not unlike that of an Olympic athlete. He told me about each killing in such poetic terms, I almost enjoyed it. But now and again, just as I was allowing myself to be pulled into his world, he would give his true nature away and I was jolted back into his violent reality. The methods he claimed to have used were horrific and he was meticulous in supplying every last lurid detail. His victims were unusually varied. Serial murderers usually have a type but he was indiscriminate in his selection. Men, women and children of all ages were included and selected at random so their deaths were a matter of chance. He refused to be coy about his motive, which was, he assured me, killing purely for the sheer pleasure of it. I watched the machine carefully as he spoke. It seemed almost alive. Lights were flashing on and off seemingly at will and at one point I could swear I heard it sigh.

Eventually Hohenheim completed his account and sat back in his chair, a self-satisfied smile on his face. 'Do you believe me?' he asked.

'It would be an extremely complex set of lies.'

'I could be seeking attention.'

'You could, but since the details of your activities will go no further, it would be a pointless quest.'

He nodded thoughtfully. 'Of course I could also kill you now.'

'Again, you could but then my colleague upstairs will alert the authorities so I wouldn't advise it.'

Hohenheim caressed his beard for a moment. 'We are alike, you and I.'

'I have never killed anyone.'

'Perhaps not, although I'm sure you have considered it.'

I blushed. He was right of course, but thinking about something and doing it are not the same things, as I reminded him.

'May I look a little more closely at your machine?' he asked as I detached him from it.

I hesitated for a moment. What if he destroyed it? But then my curiosity took over from my instinctive caution. Hohenheim approached the contraption with reverence, examining it carefully then laying his hands on it. He looked up to the ceiling and muttered something – a prayer or an incantation – it was hard to tell which. His expression was so devoid of anything human that I found myself scarcely able to breathe. I was about to make for the door to call Jim when Hohenheim relaxed.

'I must take my leave of you Dr Price. I hope your research provides what you seek.'

He smiled at my discomfort. 'I think you will find I have offered you something a little extra, Doctor. Use it well.'

Before I could ask him what he meant, he bowed slightly, picked up his coat and left. I went to the door to show him out but when I got there he had already gone. The atmosphere in the room seemed to change. I realised it had been chilly while my guest was there but now it had warmed up considerably. I looked out of the window onto Ravelin Park and laughed at my own reaction. There was nothing supernatural about Hohenheim for there he was, battling through the wind along the path to the gate, like anyone else.

There was a knock at the door and Jim poked his head round it. 'Everything all right Harry?'

I found I had a need for company so I asked him to join me for a glass of scotch.

'I see you went ahead and built the thing,' he said, looking at my contraption.

I had completely forgotten that the idea for the machine was originally his but he didn't seem at all fazed by it.

'Does it work?' he asked.

I told him about my research. It was almost a relief to share it, particularly after Hohenheim's visit. So preoccupied was I that I didn't notice it at first – a rustling sound coming from the machine.

'What's that?' Jim asked.

There it was again. It seemed to be coming from the cylinder that was supposed to gather the essence. He went over to it and peered inside.

'What is it?' I asked.

'Come and look at this.'

I did so. Inside the metal cylinder was a tiny blob of flesh. As I watched, it began to take some kind of shape, developing what looked to be limbs. Gradually it pulled itself out. It was a horrible thing – hairless and pink but warty with tiny little eyes. I leaned towards it.

'Don't touch it!' Jim cried but he was too late. The thing latched onto my hand like a leech. I felt its tiny sharp teeth sinking into my flesh as it sucked at me. I tried desperately to shake it off and Jim approached with an umbrella of all things, poking at it in an effort to loosen its grip. But it was too fast for him. It ran up my body and slipped down the back of my shirt. I could feel it scuttling around so I shrugged violently and pulled out my shirt. Then suddenly I couldn't feel it anymore.

'Where is it?' Jim asked.

'I think it's gone.'

'Best to be sure. Take off your shirt.'

'No really, it's gone.' I sank down onto an armchair and picked up my scotch. My hand was trembling.

Jim did likewise. 'What the hell was that?'

'I've no idea.'

'Do you think it'll come back? Shall I call security? No, how can I? What would I say?' he said, laughing hysterically. 'We've been attacked by a blob, about so high.'

He was starting to annoy me. 'Whatever it was, it's gone. Why don't we call it a night?'

Jim stared at me for a moment. 'Are you sure?'

'Absolutely.'

Once he'd gone I pulled off my shirt and squinted round at the mirror. There was no sign of the thing. I looked again at the cylinder. There was a dark brown viscous liquid in the bottom. I sniffed it. It smelled of peppermint and whisky. I remembered Hohenheim's words about leaving something extra and using it well. He'd certainly given me something but what was it and how should I use it?

Just as I was beginning to gather myself Jim burst through the door and started gabbling. 'I know what it was! Well I think I do. It's extraordinary. Terrifying!' He was shaking. His face was grey.

'Go on.'

'You'll never believe it!'

'Tell me!'

'I think it might be... a homunculus.'

'A what?'

'Homunculus - it's a small humanoid supposedly produced by alchemists, like Paracelsus. Didn't you say you found the papers in Turin?'

'Yes, that's where the design for the machine came from.'

'Paracelsus spent time in Turin. This could come from him!'

'What does a homunculus do?'

'Apparently it represents its creator in his purest form.'

'The question is who created it, Hohenheim or me?' I felt an itch in my lower back. Something was creeping and crawling, slowly - tiny claws - up, up, up it went onto my shoulder. I daren't move in case it attacked me with those tiny, sharp teeth. I felt it nuzzling damply on my neck and then it whispered in my ear.

'Let's hope it was you,' Jim said peering again into the machine. 'This is a remarkable find but what do we do with it? I suppose we could analyse this liquid.' He paused. 'Hang on. Did you say Hohenheim? I wonder...'

But he never got to finish his sentence. By the time I, or should I say we, had finished with him he was in no state to talk. Scream perhaps - but any conversation was limited by his lack of a tongue. My monstrous little friend ripped it out and under his instruction I finished Jim off; slowly of course, and with great invention. It was almost a shame to move the body but there was little choice. Of course I did have a good teacher - the best, you could say. I wanted to distil the essence of evil but it took Philip Hohenheim to draw it out. Little did I know that it was inside me all the time.

I have written a paper about my research but no conference will accept it. I'm an independent scholar these days. It seems the university is as short sighted as everyone else. When I speak of monsters no one believes me - until I introduce them, that is. But then of course, just like poor old Jim, they're in no position to talk.

The Boy with the Burberry Cap (Or Where the Traffic Lights Should Be)

Rebecca Swarbrick

'A Burberry cap ain't a helmet, it won't help you if you fall'
I sang to myself as I wandered to work
Thought I could hear the boy whistling too
As he cycled past me on the pavement

Until he reached the (should be) traffic lights at Devonshire
Square
Caught in the gaze of a spark- eyed man with crinkled dark hair
(His long arms, not formed from green light, but the only part of
 him that seemed to move)
And move they did
Hypnotically conducting invisible traffic, a transparent
symphony
All the lines dotted, brute violence for sympathy
The boy himself

And I stood wide-eyed and actually watched the boy sail from his
bike and fall to the ground
Under the rhythmic hands of the spark-eyed puppet man
There was a crunch on the tarmac, Burberry pulling down

And so the man smiles, waves and walks calmly away
He didn't bow to me, the one - man audience of the one act play

The boy with the Burberry cap gets back up
Unhurt
And continues with his day, slightly dazed

The cap shifts and I see a mop of blonde hair
Blue eyes that never seem to see the world around them
And I take this in as I carry on walking to Fratton station
Focused now, so as not to miss the train
And I'm humming to myself
My toy box warning call

"A Burberry cap ain't a helmet it won't help you if you fall"
And I can't help but wonder if I was ever in the audience at all.

Tide Will Tell

V H Leslie

At the edge of the city, before the noise and commotion of the motorway, a long, narrow waterway encircles the land. This grim stretch of water, merely the width of a canal, marks the city limits, a reminder to the cramped inner-city dwellers – if they ever had cause to doubt it – that the city is indeed an island. That despite the concrete and tarmac, the many bridges connecting the island to the mainland, a slim channel of seawater fills the manmade moat each day, retreating a few hours later to reveal the sludge and muck at the bottom. Here, the creek's concrete embankments speak of the control and mastery of nature, whilst the now defunct ramparts that tower behind, refer back to a time when the city's strength lay in its ability to be cut off and protected from the rest of the world.

Morgan liked to run along the periphery of the city, starting at the leisure centre and the athletics pitch, passed the lagoon and the lido before pausing at the point where Tipner Lake spilled into the creek. It wasn't a particularly picturesque route but it was as close to nature as this part of the city allowed. He wasn't the only one drawn to the water. There was always an abundance of children skirting the lake on bikes and scooters, or playing truant along the Hilsea Lines, smoking cigarettes from historic lookout spots. There were other joggers like himself, the dog walkers and cyclists, all keen to make the most of the opportunities for exercise and recreation beyond the hubbub of the city.

He'd read somewhere that exercising would increase his virility. It seemed like the least he could do with Amy having to put so many drugs in her body. But the fertility drugs made her cranky and since she'd ordered his treadmill out of the spare room and into the garage, he felt better to be out of the way entirely. He thought it was a little premature, starting to transform the spare bedroom into a baby's room, but he kept such doubts to himself. The fact was the garage was no place to exercise, amid the cobwebs and power-tools. At least here beside the creek, despite the hum of the motorway in the distance, the salt reek when the tide receded, he had space to think.

Sometimes he thought about Amy before the drugs and the hormones, or he tried to fixate on this vague idea of the child they had envisioned together, though it was blurred, like looking at something through water. He could see more clearly an image of the past, letting his imagination roam to the time when the fortifications had first been built, picturing the landscape without the motorway and the overpass, imagining people in old-fashioned clothes walking the same route he took now along the water's edge.

But he was conscious of the need to stay in the real world, at least along some of the more isolated stretches of the path, where brambles and bracken grew in abundance. A jogger had been attacked once along this route, behind the allotments where the bend of the track arched toward the water. In plain sight of the motorway, though travelling at such speed, it was hardly likely any motorist would cast more than a cursory glance toward the creek.

Morgan always ran faster along these more secluded spots, often imagining himself set upon by a masked assailant, putting up a good fight despite his aversion to violence, pumped up with adrenalin. It was good to play out these scenarios, prudent to expect danger. But it wasn't just a rational cautiousness that justified his increase in speed, or the fact that as a city boy he distrusted natural spaces, it was a feeling of unease he experienced as he drew closer to water. Oddly the spot that unnerved him most was a rather unremarkable stretch beside the roundabout, where the water disappeared beneath a bridge.

He was clearly alone with these misgivings, judging by the fact this was one of the busiest sections of the waterway, occupied by

*

Morgan walked on the spot, the belt of the treadmill turning slowly, the digitised screen broadcasting how many miles he had walked though he'd stayed in the same place. He wanted to run, but as the garage was beneath the bedroom, the reverberations proved too much of an annoyance for Amy. So he walked quietly, as if on eggshells, imagining the route beside the creek, rather than the dank, cobweb-ridden interior of the garage.

He hadn't wanted to go back to the creek. Not since he'd seen the woman on the bridge. It was enough to run the route in his mind. Starting at the leisure centre and the athletics pitch, passed the lagoon and the lido but always trying to stop short, just before the water from Tipner Lake ran beneath the bridge, before he saw the figure leaning over the railings.

It was a fruitless task. Despite his best intentions he always ended up at the bridge, gazing up at the woman. He had revisited that moment a hundred times, trying to rationalise it. The way the light had seemed to flicker and distort her, so that she looked unreal, wondering if he had conjured her entirely from his sleep-addled mind.

Amy had noticed a difference in him, she tried to encourage him to get out and about and when that had no effect, she lost her temper, blaming it on the hormones. But really he knew it was because she preferred Morgan at the periphery of her world, running circles around her. So he stayed in the garage, walking the same, worn path, day after day.

Walking wasn't so bad; he ran enough in his dreams after all. Sometimes he dreamt a masked assailant was at his heels, the kind he had imagined tackling heroically in his waking hours. But he could do little more than run in his dreams. Mostly he ran after the sack as it darted across the water, carried along in illusory currents, as if caught in churning rapids. And occasionally, despite his fear of the bridge, he raced toward it, hoping to get there before the woman cast the crying bundle she cradled into the sackcloth and over the railings and into the water.

Those times, he woke thrashing and flailing, covered in sweat, as if he had jumped into the creek.

Morgan pressed STOP and the treadmill came slowly to a halt. He wished he could stop the workings of his mind as easily. He'd walked the distance of the creek and back, along the border between reality and dream without having left the garage. It was time to return to the real world.

He made his way into the house, pausing in the kitchen to grab some refreshment, though he'd barely broken a sweat. As he reached into the fridge, he saw the pharmacy carrier bag, the open packaging splayed out on the counter top. *Clear Blue.*

'Morgan,' he heard Amy call from the bathroom. 'Morgan.'

But Morgan was out the door, running towards the creek.

*

Morgan followed the blue line of the water, running as fast as his legs allowed. He stopped at the edge of the lake, hands on his knees as he tried to steady his breathing and prevent himself from vomiting. The water was a vibrant blue, perhaps the brightest he'd ever seen it, reflecting the cloudless sky. But he knew the water wasn't clear. It might appear that way, out in the middle, beyond the rim of algae and rubbish. But there were other things in the water, impurities that left no trace but tainted the water nonetheless.

There were the tangible things that influenced the water too, stuck deep in the seabed, some of them visible when the tide retreated. The creek was a dumping ground for broken and forsaken things. Perhaps that was why it always drew so many people to its edge, those similarly damaged or redundant. Perhaps that was why the creek was the only place Morgan felt really at home.

He walked beside the water now; he'd had enough of running. He could hear children shrieking in the distance by the lido but here beside the creek he was blissfully alone. Even the ethereal woman was absent from her usual place on the bridge, though he could feel her gaze upon him regardless. And, as he approached, he could just make out the sack, floating on the water, set back within the opening of the tunnel.

This time, he didn't reach to take off his trainers. There was no need for such measures; he'd run all he needed to. Instead, he slid down the concrete embankment, the water at the bottom a cold shock as it reached his legs, then his torso. His feet sank into the silt and realising how deep it was, he broke into a swim. He felt like those adolescent boys he watched sometimes in the summer months, so carefree despite the many dangers beneath the surface.

The water was darker as he approached the underbelly of the bridge; the tide so high there was only a small gap between the water level and the roof of the tunnel. He began to tread water, edging his way toward the sack, which despite being in the water for so long, bobbed on the surface like a buoyancy aid. If only he could reach it, he knew he could stay afloat.

The current was stronger here, forming eddies around the entrance of the bridge, repelling Morgan, casting him back the way he had come, back toward home and Amy, and the slow, sad tread of his life. He could crawl out of the creek and tip the water from his trainers and run home to whatever news awaited him.

But he could also feel the undertow, the current that carried all the things unseen, the things that travelled beneath the surface. It wasn't strong enough on its own but with sufficient agitation, occasionally it could propel those secret, stifled things back to the surface.

The sack bobbed with the movement of the water, rocked as if with some internal compulsion. Morgan felt himself go under as his fingers brushed the canvas.

Undercurrent

Justin MacCormack

I think it began when I heard about the tunnels under Portsdown Hill. Standing at any high point within Portsmouth, you'll be able to see the sea to the south and the hill to the north. The chalk hill, its solemn white face and old military forts speckled along its top, was always looking over the city and making me curious to see what secrets it held. With the type of military history that Portsmouth has, it didn't take a genius to see that the hill was bound to be the centre of many urban legends; after all, the talk of hidden bunkers somewhere deep inside the hill couldn't be just idle rumour. How could I resist the temptation?

Urban exploration wasn't a major thing until I was already in my early twenties. The hobby hadn't hit the mainstream media yet, so it was mostly kept to online bulletin boards and websites. People from all corners of the world would post and chat together, discussing locations that were abandoned, forgotten about or otherwise left to decay, and we would share photographs. Hospitals were very popular. I was into the abandoned hotels that people had photographed from Russia. Those were amazing – entire buildings which had been left behind when the nobility fled. Castles and Manor Houses and everything in between, left in perfect condition, untouched by time. Those websites were where I met two of my closest friends.

Al was the first person on the website that I really got talking to. He used the online name 'End of the Line', which suited his love of railway sites. Dave, on the other hand, was the archetypal military fan. His thing was the army. He was the type who had a massive collection of military surplus. His big kick in urban exploration was the unused bases or naval forts, that sort of thing. We planned the first expedition for almost three weeks, reading all the reports we could find. Dave covered most of the military Intel on the forts and bunkers in and around Portsdown Hill, and it wasn't long before we were ready to head in. The experience was exhilarating. We moved past the walled-off entryways and climbed down a series of old rusted ladders into a network of barren tunnels that spread in every direction. The passageways were littered with dust and small accrued stones, lined with naval grey walls and heating pipes. I wanted to believe that the location had been untouched since the cold war, but I knew this couldn't be true, that other explorers had walked these tunnels. We stuck close behind Al as he led the way, taking photographs as he went.

When we got to the rooms, Dave was in his glory. They had been stripped, consoles and documents had been removed when the base was vacated, but some of the furnishings remained. Bunk beds in the sleeping quarters, old-style kitchen cookers in the mess halls, desks and chairs in the command centres. They were all present and accounted for, and were photographed for posterity. When we left we felt as if we had walked many miles; we were tired, exhausted but satisfied. We began to plan our next expedition immediately. It was Al who had the idea and presented it to the two of us – he had heard the rumours for a while, and wanted to strike it big.

'We should check out the Nelson tunnels,' he told us one evening while we were sharing a dinner of take-away chicken. I wasn't too sure what the Nelson tunnels actually were, and even Dave only had a few scraps of information, and the websites seemed to be incomplete in their knowledge of them. The tunnels were so named for their proximity to the trail that Nelson himself had made through the city. Four people on the website had attempted it, but only half-heartedly. The entrance for the tunnels was easy enough to get to, located less than fifteen minutes from Clarence Pier. But it came with its own particular hazard which most explorers simply didn't care for. The water levels within the tunnels could vary, rising with the tides, and this made planning the exploration extremely difficult. The website boasted a series of photographs, but none of them were especially good, and they only ever mapped the first chamber. For most people, the risk versus reward was simply too far out of balance, and so the Nelson tunnels was almost forgotten even by our community. Naturally, Al loved the idea. I wasn't personally sold on it, until I realised if we were to be the first people to fully map out the network, the popularity we'd achieve on the website would be staggering. I would become a success story, not just in our little group of three, but within an entire online community. So I said yes, it sounded like a wonderful idea. It was agreed, we'd hit the tunnels.

We hurried along down across the common and found the gate set into the embankment without any trouble. The website had called it a doorway, but in reality it was more a set of metal railings formed into a gateway. Dave made quick work of the latch on it. He was wearing a full backpack, decked with every tool that we were likely to need, including a manhole key. He pulled the key out and inserted it to the manhole cover, pulling the circular covering free with a heavy grinding sound. We peered inside to see the tunnel descending downwards, with row upon row of metal hand-rails set as ladders into the damp walls. One by one, we worked our way downwards.

I was the last to get down the ladders, and the ground was wet beneath my shoes. About half an inch of sea water remained in the chamber and the strong smell of salt filled the air. Al was already switching on his torch, allowing us to see the area around us. The walls seemed to be made of hard-packed concrete, trailing off into the distance. As we started to walk, we noticed that beneath the light splashing of our footsteps there was a dull crunch. The ground beneath the water was etched with pebbles and grit. This was good, as it meant that our steps were significantly less likely to slide and result in a fall.

The tunnel went onwards for what must have been ten minutes, gradually turning to the left as it did so. Dave pointed out that the route that we were taking would wind us up along the coast of the beach, leaning slightly towards the sea. Al said that the tunnel was on a rather slight decline, very slowly tilting downwards as we progressed. I asked him if he thought that the tunnel could have been used as part of the sewage system for the city, but he doubted it, telling us that the construction of the tunnels was all wrong for such a use. There was a soft groan in the tunnel's echoing background, a dull rumbling which I recognised as the reverberating bass hum of distant water. We knew that the tunnel must somewhere empty out into the sea. We were so busy photographing the tunnels that we almost walked right past the metal door that was set into the wall of the tunnel.

When Al pointed out the door, we pressed around to examine it. It was solid, without any markings or signs posted on it, and it didn't even have a handle to open it. When I knocked on it, there was a resounding echo from the other side. It didn't take long for the three of us to decide that we wanted to push through, and thankfully Dave had just the right tool for the job. He held out a thin length of metal that I thought resembled a crowbar, but Dave called a latch key. It didn't take him two minutes to ease the door open. Beyond it, we found another sheer drop, falling into the depths below. Small metal rungs hung on the wall, giving us a clear way down if we wanted to. We turned to one another and discussed the prospect of pushing onwards. We had already come far, and pushing onwards into this deeper tunnel would surely be extremely dangerous.

It was decided between us all that if we were to make the trip down the rungs, we should take even greater care in doing so. Dave, as prepared as he always was, had a length of rope with him. We decided that the first one of us to head down should tie the rope around his waist. If he latched a knot from the rope onto each rung as he went, it would ensure that if any of us were to fall the rope would catch us. Al went first, tying the rope around his waist. He made his way down the ladder, rung by rung, taking his time to secure his way as he went. When he reached the bottom, he called up to me, and I pulled his side of the rope back up and fastened it around myself. I worked my way down; noticing just how wet the rungs felt. Half-way down, I told Al that I thought it would be a good idea to leave the rope there, in case we started to run out of time and had to make our way out in a hurry. He was midway through agreeing when I had to pause to wipe some seaweed off of my fingers. I reached the ground and passed the rope back up to Dave.

As Dave made his way down, I took the time to examine the new chamber. Unlike the one above, the walls there didn't seem to be made of concrete, or any kind of natural material that I could determine. They felt wet to the touch, and hard and somewhat cold, and I thought that we must have found our way into a natural cavern of some sort. I hadn't been paying attention when it happened. One moment I was scanning the new chamber with my torch, and the next a scream split the air. By the time I had turned around, all I was able to see was Dave colliding with the ground. I knew immediately that he had fallen – no, there was a clattering roar that broke the echoes of his fall, telling me that one of the rungs had given way. We hurried over to Dave; he was on his side on the ground, a tangled spread of army camouflage jeans and backpack. He was gasping heavily, letting loud cries of pain out in strong bellows. That was when we noticed his leg, bent double under him, its angle sharply leaning inwards towards his body in a manner it surely shouldn't. I brushed Al to one side and took a look at the leg; it wasn't a simple break, I could see that much. From just above his ankle, a large bulge protruded from beneath his skin, indicating that the bone had snapped and threatened to rupture.

Dave lay back against the wet rocky ground, struggling to catch his breath. Al was already on his mobile phone, struggling to call for an ambulance. I spoke to Dave loudly, telling him to stay calm, that it wasn't as bad as it looked. It was a problem, yes, but a manageable one. Al started to swear, and when I looked over I seen him shaking his mobile frantically.

'No signal' he replied, and asked if I could try mine. I shook my head, I didn't even have mine with me – I've always disliked carrying mobile phones. We reached into Dave's pocket to try to recover his, hoping that his signal would work better in the subterranean tunnel. When I pulled Dave's phone free, I found that the screen was smashed. The damn thing wouldn't even turn on. I threw it on the ground.

'Okay,' I said. 'We're going to carry you out of here. Al, can you unfasten the rope?' I planned to put together a makeshift harness, carry Dave up the ladder into the tunnel above, and from there we were only one step into the city again.

That was when Al pointed out the rungs that lay broken on the ground. I had thought that there was just one, probably old and rusted from the sea salt. I was wrong – it was all of the ones that the rope had been tied to. Each one had been ripped clear from the crumbling old cave wall and lay in a contorted pile in the torchlight.

We both tried to figure out a way to get back into the upper tunnel. We spent almost half an hour trying to climb it by hand, or to force the rungs back into place. None of our attempts yielded any success. Dave was breathing heavily, struggling to bite back the pain he was in. He started talking about his girlfriend, about how much he wanted to see her again. I was single, I had nobody except these two guys with me, and I sure as hell wanted to get us out of there together. And all the time, we were thinking about the clock, about how long it'd be before the water started to make its way into the tunnel.

Without any other ideas, we pulled Dave up onto one foot and took his weight between the two of us, supporting him on our shoulders, and tried to make our way onwards into the tunnel. I don't know how long we walked for over that crunching, wet pebbled ground, carrying Dave between the two of us. After a while, his pain started to ease – I suspect his endorphins had kicked in, perhaps. He didn't talk about his leg or the pain, but would repeat over and over that he wanted to see his girlfriend, he just wanted to get out of these tunnels and see her, that he didn't want to die without seeing her. We both told him again and again that he wasn't going to die. That only happened in the movies. In real life people like us stumbled out of the caves and got found by the coastguard.

I don't know how long we walked for. The tunnels seemed to turn at different angles, leaning left for a while and then turning sharply to the right. Al, who had until now been able to tell exactly where we should have been, eventually confessed that he had no idea where we were. This announcement brought a new stream of cries from Dave, who began to sob and repeat in fear.

'We're going to die down here. We're going to die down here.' I told him again that we weren't, but in all honesty, at this point even I wasn't sure that was the truth. We continued onwards, unsure if we were making any progress at all, not knowing if we were directly under the city or beneath the sea now. My feet started to hurt from the walking, and before long we had to stop to eat. We didn't have many snacks; Dave had brought a few chocolate bars and a tub of ready-made pasta which we shared between us. It was starting to feel very cold in the tunnels. That was when Al finally asked me to step to one side with him, leaving Dave to finish the pasta. We stepped a few feet further down into the tunnel, and Al leaned close to me and whispered something to me, something that I think all three of us had been dimly aware of but had been too afraid to say out loud – the water should have come in an hour ago.

We pushed on, not daring to mention the time that Al's phone was showing, or the risk of the water. We walked in silence now, with only Dave's moaning breaths to keep the silence from being complete. I don't know how long we walked on for; time itself seemed to lose all sense of meaning, our anxiety keeping us from wanting to see it. I grew tired; my eyes became sore, my feet shuffling rather than walking. When Al slipped and fell, causing the rest of us to collapse onto the wet ground, we decided that we should rest for a while. We slept. I couldn't say how long for, only that it was fitful and uncomfortable, with only the silence for company. But in the middle of that sleep, I woke. The other two were asleep, but something troubled me, and I knew what it was. A dull sound, somewhere too quiet to be heard even under the white sound of the silence; somewhere in the depths of the cave, perhaps, or maybe I was hearing my own heartbeat.

We awoke and continued onwards. As the hours pressed on, the three of us found that we had less and less to speak about, so we walked in silence. What could we say to keep each other's spirits up? None of us wanted to look at the clock on Al's phone to see how long we had really been down there, afraid that the time would consume us. We were hungry, all of us. I thought that when we got out of there, I'd get myself a huge dinner. We slept again. We walked onwards. Al didn't speak, he simply pushed on, and pausing only to make sure his torch was strong enough to see the way ahead. Dave, when he did speak, only mumbled about how he wanted to see his girlfriend again – he was looking pale, his eyes seemed dark. Sometimes, all he could manage was to say her name to him again and again in a near whisper. The third time we slept, and I was once more awakened by the sense of the sound of my own heartbeat. I took the chance to sneak a look at Al's phone. We had been down there almost four days.

Dave didn't wake up that day.

We had tried to wake him up. Al had been shaking him, screaming at him to wake up. Neither of us knew what to do. The entire moment seemed more like something out of a dream; I had to check to make sure I wasn't asleep. I didn't want to move on. I had never, in my entire life, lost a friend or family member to death before. Al was certain that it was due to infection, but I couldn't understand that – there had been no puncture of the skin. We almost argued about it, but neither of us could manage to fight. Fighting between the two of us just didn't seem important anymore.

Neither of us knew what we should do. The ground felt too hard to bury him, and we didn't have anything else we could do. God, we just left him there. What else could we have done? I hated myself for doing it, but we just left him there. Al took his backpack, which we dug through to find something to eat, but there wasn't anything there we could use. We just left him there, and continued down the tunnels.

We found Dave's mobile phone later that day. I didn't even see it;

all I heard was this glass-like cracking noise as I walked. And there it was, broken on the ground beneath my foot. I couldn't even think straight – I picked it up, walked over to Al and demanded to know why it was there. How could it have been there? It wasn't possible. We had left it behind, at the entrance to the tunnel, along with the broken rungs. The rungs, which lay scattered at the foot of the wall not far from where we now stood. That was when I lost it. I screamed at Al, launching myself at him, trying to punch him with the last scraps of my strength.

'You bastard!' I screamed, 'You've been leading us around in circles!' Al was screaming, shouting back at me, and telling me that it was impossible. But I couldn't stop, not after what had happened that morning and not after having left Dave's body behind. It was his entire fault, it had to be. He was our leader; he was the most experienced one. He was meant to know what he was doing! If he hadn't made such a cock-up of this, Dave would still be alive. I wanted to make Al regret it, I wanted him to pay for this mess, and so I punched him again and again, driving my fist against him. I don't know if he was bleeding or if it was just the wetness of the cavern itself. Soon I had exhausted myself and collapsed, my entire body soaked.

When we could both stand again we continued down the tunnels. Neither of us wanted to mention what had just happened. As Al nursed his jaw and bloodied nose, neither of us could think of anything further to say. We stumbled as we walked, feeling weaker. I think, gradually, we were starting to starve. I couldn't tell, not really. I didn't feel as hungry anymore, but my legs shook as I walked. We slept twice as we continued on, and I started to think that the time between each bouts of sleep was growing shorter. Twice, I woke from my sleep certain that the sound of my heartbeat was thumping out in the echo of the tunnels.

Two days after Dave had died, we found ourselves in a part of the tunnel that seemed entirely unusual. The ground beneath us gave slightly, a little like mud. The walls themselves felt wetter to the touch, and we both thought that at this point in the cavern network

Cracked City

James Bicheno

'Don't step on the cracks. If you step on the cracks, you're dead.'
Remember that? The warning that got passed down the line as
you walked, two-by-two, on school trips around the city? The
superstition your class mates received from older children and
passed down to youngsters stays in mind as you go through life. As
you make the same journeys around town, your feet learn where the
cracks in the pavement are. As you go up in shoe size, they turn as if
of their own accord, so as not to disturb the lines of cement that
bridge the granite slabs together.

You walk alone, the only sounds being the odd crow or your
shoes tapping along the winding streets. Your route is lit by a
distant sun, half hidden in a winter sky, white with a hint of blue.
Along the way you pass skeletons of trees, once rich, green and full
of life, then browned and snatched away by autumn, now husks at
the mercy of the elements. The only signs of nature in this pale city
of blocks.

Humankind has dominated the landscape as far as the eye can see
and beyond. The square miles that surround you are covered with
evidence of the successes and failures of the constant evolution of
engineering. Nature has been removed, driven away or buried under
tarmac tracks and granite tessellations.

But what would happen if you stepped on the cracks? That was
the question no one seemed to know the answer to. Would you
damage the pavement, causing further cracks to appear? Would you
be struck by lightning or would you fall through them? Does
something lurk beneath the pavement? Is there life beneath the

otherwise dead ground, intent on pushing through any weakness in the solid stones?

You remember those programmes on the TV? The ones that talk about lost and abandoned cities that fall victim to the forests and jungles that surround them. Within months, years, of people leaving, Nature takes revenge. Buildings are fettered by weeds and creepers, works of art are swallowed up and the ground is broken up from below. Cracks spread far and wide along the ground, forming their own mosaics between the natural and unnatural. And these cracks spread up through the buildings, making them brittle and unstable.

And what would that mean if a foot slipped and disturbed the cement lining?

Do you step on the cracks now?

Basements

Matt Parsons

The house on King's Road is the oldest building in the street. I
think that was why I always felt uncomfortable there. All the other
buildings in the street were modern: 1980s flats, contemporary
offices, a Tesco Metro, a Co-op, a pizza takeaway, a vape shop, a
kebab shop, and so on. You could imagine all these other buildings
nudging each other and muttering resentfully. What's that old
Victorian building doing there, anyway? What right does it have to
be there?

I'd been lodging at the house for a couple of months, when the
landlord, Mr Curtain, met with an accident. I came home one day
around six o'clock and found him at the foot of the stairs, bruised,
bleeding, and delirious. The ambulance crew who took him away all
looked similar, as though they might be brothers. I heard them
talking to each other outside while they smoked, and I couldn't
understand a word. Mr Curtain often complained about the number
of foreign people in the street. He said he could walk down King's
Road from one end to the other and not hear a word of English. It
was a lie. He was a bad tempered, miserable, bony old man. As the
ambulance pulled away, I was running my fingers along the top of
the door, looking for the key to Mr Curtain's rooms.

I realise I am not painting a flattering picture of myself, but there
was a very good reason for my behaviour. You see, Mr Curtain was
hiding something, and I wanted to know what it was. He had always
taken great pains to make very sure that I could never see into his
rooms. He always opened the door just enough to peer out with one
eye, and if I surprised him while he was leaving the room he would

quickly retreat back inside. But the most curious thing was that there were noises coming from the room, even when Mr Curtain was out: echoing, banging noises, and muffled voices, as though someone was trying to attract my attention. I suspected Mr Curtain was keeping someone captive.

Mr Curtain owned a number of properties. I don't know where he actually lived, but he spent a lot of time in that room in the house on King's Road. He'd arrive before nine in the morning and stay until late. He'd shuffle to the shop on the corner several times a day, and while he was out, I'd listen at the door. Then he caught me looking through the keyhole. He'd come back to get an umbrella, and he saw me through the front door window. He was furious and accused me of plotting to steal from him. He'd always seemed to regret his decision to let the upstairs rooms to me, and he was obviously determined to take the first opportunity to evict me. I'd signed a contract, but that evening we agreed I would leave the house. The next day he fell down the stairs.

I knew despite his obsessive secrecy, he sometimes left a spare set of keys on the architrave above the door to his rooms. I'd never had the courage to use them. Now was my chance. I felt a thrill as I turned the key in the lock. I knew it was wrong, but I also knew that Mr. Curtain would probably never leave the hospital, so there was very little danger I would be discovered. I opened the door and switched the light on. What I saw was not at all what I was expecting to see. I'd pictured gas lamps, Victoriana, Persian rugs, grandfather clocks, maybe the odd stuffed animal, that sort of thing. It would have been in keeping with the house, and with Mr Curtain himself. Disappointingly, much of the furniture was poor quality flat-pack. The floor was covered in threadbare, heavy duty charcoal carpet tiles, and the walls were painted a bland oatmeal colour. There were boxes of copier paper, coffee stained mugs, overflowing bins and desk tidies full of highlighter pens everywhere. An old calendar hung on the wall.

It wasn't the sort of place anyone could live in. It was an office. There was a musty smell, and more than the usual amount of dust you'd expect to find in an old house which is never cleaned. I once read somewhere that dust is mainly composed of dead skin. I know it's not really true, but somehow, the idea that this particular dust was made of dead, grey skin seemed plausible. I ran my finger along the table and left a trail. Then I heard a thump. It seemed to come from the basement. I knew there couldn't be anyone living down there by choice. It would have been too small. There would have been no power down there, and it would have been too damp. I headed towards the basement door. I took a deep breath and opened it.

The stairs were carpeted, there was woodchip wallpaper, and there was a strip light. I crept down the steps. I could hear the noises again. There was another door at the bottom of the stairs, so I took another deep breath, and threw the door open. I was expecting to discover a bound and gagged prisoner, but all I found was more office space. The place still smelled of paint and new carpet. A light flickered overhead. I felt dizzy. I don't know whether the paint fumes were affecting me, but my head was spinning from the discovery that the basement was larger than the ground floor.

At this point I was beginning to feel afraid. I was about to turn around and leave, when I saw another door. Above it was a gold-coloured plastic plaque, which said EXIT in black capital letters. I listened at the door. I heard nothing. I decided that the plaque must be lying. No doubt, the door led to a store cupboard. I opened the door and found another flight of steps. The smell of fresh paint was even stronger, with an undertone of filler and cement. I descended, and the door shut behind me. There must have been a concealed closing mechanism. There was no handle on the inside of the door. I scrabbled at it, trying to prise it open, but it was no use. I tried to force it open with a key, but my hands were sweating, and I was trembling. I wanted to bang on the door and shout for help, but I couldn't. What if there was someone down below? Would they hear me? What would happen then? I checked my phone. There was no signal, of course, as I was too far underground. It seemed there was no way back. I had to press on.

I'll spare you the details of how many basements I progressed through. I lost count. Every few floors, a door would softly close behind me with a click, and I'd be unable to open it. I encountered an old fax machine and an ancient beige PC. Both were switched on. I tried the telephone, but there was no dial tone. There were other signs of habitation too. Every now and then I'd find dirty mugs, overflowing ashtrays, and pictures in frames. There was never anyone in the picture, just badly lit, badly composed, out of focus shots of similar bland office spaces.

When at last I did encounter a human being, I grabbed a steel ruler to defend myself. The man was confused. He muttered something I couldn't understand, and pointed at the door which, inevitably, led down to another level. From then on I encountered more people. None of them acknowledged me. They were all too occupied with stirring their tea, eating biscuits, and staring at screens. I watched some of them at work. They were doodling, or filling word documents with random letters.

I sat on a swivel chair and tried to work out what was happening to me. I came to the conclusion that I must either have been drugged, or that I was experiencing a particularly bad, particularly vivid waking dream. One thing which was becoming clear was that with each level, the office space was becoming more salubrious. It was as though I was progressing through the history of modern office space as I descended deeper and deeper into the earth. By the time I entered a space resembling a contemporary office - the sort of place a fancy hipster web design company would occupy - the humans I encountered were naked, hunched, mono-browed, Neanderthal looking creatures. I was crying, and I was too paralysed by fear to resist them when they crowded around me, lifted me up, and carried me down the final flight of stairs.

The floors were smooth and grey and the walls were clad in brushed steel. Paper thin laptop screens cast a blue light. I was brought before a pair of steel doors, above which glowed an orange, arrow shaped light. I cried out, gibbering senselessly. I had been brought before a lift, and now something was coming up to meet me. One by one, the computer screens around me began to dim. I struggled to free myself from the grip of these degenerate office workers, but it was too late. In the half-light of the sleeping computers, I heard a ping, saw the metal doors slide open, and felt a light breeze issue from the open lift shaft.

How can I describe what emerged? I cannot bear to think of it... yet I cannot stop thinking of it. I suppose it was the force not of nature, but of progress. It was utterly inhuman. I don't know how I escaped, or how long it took me. I sometimes dream of kicking down fire doors and scrambling up narrow, fluorescently lit staircases. I do remember emerging into the night air and running out into the street, screaming.

I never returned to the house on King's Road, but I understand the council has since been informed of the unauthorised extension, and filled it in with concrete.

Imprints on the Air

Helen Salsbury

I'm closeted between glass and window blind, looking out, looking down. The blind, which rests against my back, prevents the sunlight from glaring across the computer screen on the far wall, prevents Ian from muttering at me from his nest on the sofa. The scent from my day at the shop – a confused mix of flower essences – exudes from my pores, finds no way through the panes of the full length window, rises to the narrow apex where blind and double-glazing meet.

From here I can see both sea and land. The water merges in and out between the buildings, between the different strips of land. The people below me are small figures in a geometric world. Even the whale tail statue which plunges down into concrete is made small from twelve floors up. When I first stood here, before our blinds were fitted, the fall away in front of me was giddying; a pleasurable vertigo. I miss it now that the months have passed and I have become accustomed.

The blinds, which Ian purchased from an internet site, are silvery white, and these are the colours which pass through them into our apartment.

A soundless force pushes a cloud over the sun. This brief shade lasts just long enough for me to slip unobserved from behind the blind, into the constant hum of our open plan lounge/kitchen. He's on the sofa. As the sun is unveiled, the filtered light shimmers with silver dust motes and casts its customary spell on my vision.

This is what I see: silver cables move tendon-like, muscle-like, down from Ian's shoulders to power his shiny, silver hands, each finger curling and uncurling as he types. On his right hand a silver bird is etched, wings folded. The computer screen displays the composite pieces of his personality. Columns and rows of monitoring windows, each with its own status light, a coloured border which shows blue when there's no crisis and red when there is. In the central window is the larger rectangle of his constant search. His followers are hungry, he needs always to feed them. Is it them who suck him in?

'Where do you go?' My words flutter through the air towards him.

'What did you say?' It's a mutter, a half-fragment of attention. But the screen flashes behind his eyes, and the flow of him is into and through the screen, out – who knows where?

A hint of rose seeps from me – distinguishable from the other scents. My eyes glance off the silver shine of close-shaved skull which envelops his half-man, half-machine brain; I shut my lids and picture blond hair falling forward as he bends to sniff my scent. This is how we met.

He had a tattoo of a bird in the crook between his thumb and finger, black lines against pale skin. As he held my wrist, the wings of the bird opened. He bent forward and the tip of his nose, cool from the outside air, pushed against the beat of my pulse; it quickened.

Cold silver nails tap away.

I sink into a chair. I watch the pulse of his attention. The reach between him and the screen. But no, that's not right. It's beneath the screen, that's where he's talking really. That silver box which hums, that strange lozenge-shaped object with its flashing 'I'm okay' lights, with its cables which lead into the wall.

Is that where he goes?

In mythology the hero follows the heroine into Hades, wrestles for her soul. He's made me a princess in a tower, but perhaps I would rather be a hero.

He tweeted an article recently about astral projection. Not his words, someone else's. That's how it works. But the article was interesting, just like so many of them are. I leave my body in the chair, and move my essence towards the cable.

There's a gritty tightness where it feeds through the wall. I slip through the plastic insulation into the telephone-wire copper. It's like a dual tramway, pulses speeding in both directions. I'm for the down elevator. It whooshes me out of the apartment towards the centre of our floor: dark doors and soft clean carpet and lifts. Companion cables join mine from the other apartments; I have to cling to know which is mine. We pour downwards, growing stronger, past the left over echo of a seagull who got trapped during the tower's construction ten years ago. She's full of anger and hunger and a tug so strong to her nesting young that I want to follow. But if I left this cable highway could I find my way back?

The ground floor. I sense a whirl of energy around the concierge's desk. It's the place where the apartment dwellers meet, where some of us linger to chat, to hear about the history under our feet: the naval training school that used to be here, and before that the mill pond, and before that the sea. The concierge's desk is where we become less separate, just briefly, each day. The copper cable pours on, down into the locked basement. A cupboard, a slotting in, a joining. Not one, but many.

Scared, but riding. Where do you go?

The massed power of us leaves the cupboard, rushes through the ground, a noisy power-surge. It's too fast, too strong.

I jump out of the cable.

I'm still underground, but where?

Keep still – listen, sense, find your bearings.

At first I think it's the internet current I sense, still speeding, but it's cooler and there are bubbles within it. White foam. Rushing water, turning and tripping over a wheel. Constant.

But when? There's no water here now.

Are you the mill pond from the past? How many years were you here?

Centuries, that's how it feels. Like it was here for centuries.

Then what happened?

The sliding slither of mud and stone, filling in, the water spilling up and out, and all around small, wriggling darts of swimming things, trapped, smothered, crushed.

I feel it too now, the weight. I escape upwards like the water.

Grass and mud shimmers through the concrete present. I follow it. The naval training school, the playing fields.

It's full of running, rushing, masculine energy. Chasing a ball, chasing each other, leaping and fighting and laughing. It's fun. Sweat, heat, the intense now of competition. In the background there's a plume of smoke from a thick cigar, an arrogant man leaning casually against thin air, his gaze making a slow up, down and through appraisal of me. Then there's jazz, and a sensation of digging, the crackle of a loudspeaker somewhere in the background calling a man's name.

All this energy, all these fragments, like imprints on the air, drawing me in, drawing me close.

They sense me. Masculine energy jostles in to sniff.

Who are you? You're not a ghost. You smell of flowers.

Am I afraid?

No, don't be. Look we're digging trenches, but we're avoiding the football fields. We're ahead of the game, the way we always are. We checked out all the shovels from the dockyard days ago. We anticipated the Munich crisis, the order to dig.

Happy, that's how I feel them. The jazz music, the men digging, the bright pulses of memory.

Are you ghosts?

I don't ask. It's like mist on a mountain down here, the way back beginning to fade. I need to reverse, I need to find the current of electricity, need to ride it back up.

I pull away, not listening to the *don't go, don't go,* hardly hearing the *come back soon.*

There it is. I'm weak, tired. But the strong current of the Internet is just in front of me. I push through into it. Riding the up elevator, separating away from the other apartments, crawling out onto our carpet, creeping back to my body, looking across to where the silver

hybrid is tapping, tapping, tapping away.
Come back soon.

*

The Lipstick Tower can be seen from many places in Portsmouth, always with the spindle of the Spinnaker Tower close by: the two tall markers of my world. A city within a city, a place within a place. When I see them as I'm travelling towards, I get a sense of homecoming; that's where I live.

*

'It stinks in here.' The first words Ian ever said to me.
Not so romantic, but factual.
I'd seen him outside the window working the retail outlet's central square, the cocky way he approached customers, a screen of some sort in his hands, the way he stepped back and kept talking as he tried to persuade, to capture their attention. The slump of defeat as they detoured past. The regroup.
After a couple of hours he entered the fragrances shop.
'Looking for a present for my girlfriend.'
Not jealous at all – honest.
'Plus, I need a break from the indifference.'
I'd offered complicity, 'Customers!' and taken serious time to help him choose.
'Can I test it on you?' he'd asked.

*

At night the arc of the Lipstick Tower's top is rimmed with a blue light. The same blue as the monitoring lights on the computer screen.

*

Two weeks later he came back. 'The perfume smelt better on you.'

During lunch breaks we'd leave the red-brick commercial wharf via the modern entrance which tunnelled below the train line. We'd walk beside the car filled road, with its noise and dirt, then turn and enter the residential wharf through the old, square turreted, wide arched gate; pausing to allow fictitious naval guards to check our credentials, their navy uniforms far darker than the sky. Even though the two wharfs were directly linked by an internal walkway, we always took this long route round.

The Lipstick Tower climbed up on our left as we walked through. We headed past it, alongside the ornamental stub of bridged-across canal – three flat sections of flowing water – to the marina at the concourse end. Once there, we'd lean against the railings and look back, our gazes lifting up – oval floor by oval floor of glass.

'If we lived there, we'd own the sky.' He took my hand, bird feathers unfurling.

*

We had a home each, a parent each, a single bed each. We started saving up to leave.

He went on a couple of Internet marketing courses to learn how to make a bit on the side. 'It's about catching people's attention, building followers. It takes time. You have to keep talking to them, finding new things to say, trawling the Internet for snippets of information, inspiration, entertainment.'

At first he was just the one personality, then gradually many.

'I've got more followers than Beckham,' he'd told me.

It takes time. A year: 'I'm getting there.' Then another: 'Close your eyes.'

The sound of traffic in my ears as he leads me, blindly, through a rotating door, over soft carpet, into a whoosh of lift.

'I've only got enough for a few months rent, so far.'

And then the surprise: the open-to-the-sky apartment, the pleasurable vertigo.

And his gradual turn into silver.

*

It becomes easier to follow the flow of the current down to the basement, out through the cool ghost-shadow of the mill pond, up to the football ground. I'm building confidence, ready – sometime soon – to venture into the Internet world, to find Ian and bring him back.

But not just yet.

Once I rescue him, I will have to give this up – the energy, the sheer leaping physical joy, the crowding shouldering mass of ghosts, the fragments of their stories: the places they've seen, the women they've loved, the machines they've controlled.

They cluster and clamour for my attention. And I've never been this popular.

*

'Where do you go?' The silver hybrid asks, fingertips paused on the keyboard. 'Where do you go when you sit in that chair?'

I notice an unfamiliar taste in my mouth, push my stiff body up and onto its feet, head into the kitchen: pans unused, a cardboard box on the surface, wood-fired pizza from the Tesco convenience store just across from our tower – he's been outside! – dirty plates.

When I sit back down, there's a different window on the top right corner of the flat screen. It monitors me. I look at the light which rims it: blue, steady; then I slide into the cable and slip away.

*

A football field and men digging to the sound of jazz.

We are digging trenches, but we're avoiding the football fields.

Pride.

We checked out all the shovels from the dockyard. We were ahead of the game, like always.

Happy, that's how I feel them. The jazz music, the men digging, the bright pulses of memory.

A loudspeaker calls out a man's name.

'That was it,' a young ghost voice, much fainter than some, 'That was my draft chit. My first ever.'

He sidles into me like soft fog – an image flashes: racing up a gangplank, kit heavy on back, shoulder to shoulder with bigger men, older men.

'Five days out and just stopped throwing up.'

I taste bile.

'That was when...' His voice trembles.

Other voices, jumping on top of him. The music grows louder – the young ghost on the gangplank fades.

'You're drowning him out! Stop it. I want to listen. Don't be so mean.'

It's not good to say. We don't talk about it. He'll frighten you away. You won't come here any more.

But the fog of him is still there: trembling inside me.

'Tell me.'

A dolphin shape in the water, but too cylindrical, too fast, so fast that time has slowed. Impact. Flung down. Burning diesel smell. Searing heat. Is it me screaming? Roasting smell.

I never thought it would be me. Not me. Not me.

'It's okay,' I say.

I wanted my mother.

Ian and I have never discussed children.

'I'm here.'

The curl of him inside my body.

*

The others are crowding, clustering. Masculine energy damped, hope risen.

'You want to tell? You need to tell?'

I am the eternal mother. They, damp and fuzzy phantasms, draw into me.

The Malayan Emergency. The motor launch pulling into the river, 'Keep down, snipers on the bank.' A canister rolling. Moving to stop it, breaking cover. Fist into my chest, fist into my stomach, two rifle cracks. I'm down. Sky heaving.

Not me. Not me.

The flat beach, the flat sea, the enemy mine smelling of salt water. Nostrils incredibly keen, vision bright, fingers steady. War winning secrets inside, another medal possible. Tiny click. Booby trapped. Turn to run. Blown. Scattered thumps.

Which bit of me is me?

Deep sea, belly of the Russian ship above me, taste of cigar and whisky in my mouth, girl's kiss on my lips, 'piece of cake - done it so many times', hugged from behind by frogman arms, one of which lifts - a silver gleam - wrestles towards my throat, this strange embrace, piercing pain, dark red cumulus massing in front of me, growing as I dwindle.

Not me. Too bloody right not me! Never me.

Prison camp: empty belly, empty mind, fever. I can't remember home any more. Fading and slipping, quietly, like a whisper - not me.

The Korean War, the Indonesian Confrontation, the Falklands, explosions, fires, trapped under broken off ship, drownings.

And me - I was an accident - it wasn't even war. But even so.

Not me.

Not me.

Not me.

*

In the fragrances shop a customer has to ask me twice.

The many deaths are static within me, badly connected wires, buzzing.

The flowers speak. *Fluttering layered corpses, constricted,*

compressed, the juices squeezed out of us – bleeding colour, weeping colour.
There's too many of you! Is there nothing left?
Just this: a glass bottle, the rasp of a stopper removed.
'I've dabbed on so many different scents,' the customer says, 'I can't tell the difference. Can I try it on you?'
Not me. Not me.
I give her a narrow white rectangle of card and she tilts the bottle.
The flower ghosts soak into the white.

*

I'm closeted between glass and window blind, looking out, looking down. A badly-mixed scent – essence of dead flowers – seeps from my pores, finds no way through the window panes, rises to the narrow apex where blind and double-glazing meet.
I open the top half of the window, chest high.
It's raining, and the whale tale plunging into concrete is made realistic by the wet.
What is the moment of separation? The severing of the string?
The blind rests against the back of my head, my shoulders, my bottom. The blind is pale, but I am paler. The many deaths have thinned me out, turned me translucent, made me light enough to fly.
The blind is jerked away. In the water-backed mirror of the window a figure is displayed and behind him a screen. The square in the top right corner is rimmed with a bright red light. As the water runs, it wavers.
'Don't go,' he says.
'I wanted to build you a palace,' he says.
'Wanted to earn enough that we could stay here forever,' he says.
When I asked the ghosts why so many of them were gathered on the football field, why they hadn't lingered with lovers or family, they said, *We were happy here.*
'I did it for you,' he says.

But I don't turn, because if I do I will see the fractured look in his eye, and I will remember the many deaths, the point of separation. And yet, I notice that the hand on my shoulder has the pallor of human skin in winter time, and my gaze touches on the etched silver lines of a bird whose wings have not yet spread.

The fall away in front of me is giddying. A pleasurable vertigo.

Still Dark Water

Nick Morrish

I – The Sea Kayaker

4th January 2016

We launched into still dark water by the shelter of Whale Island. Even in the harbour, the sea is seldom calm, but at night, just occasionally, the water is completely still and the surface feels slow and glutinous, like molten glass or molasses.

'QHM, QHM, QHM. This is Kayak Group PCC. Seven kayaks requesting permission to cross from Whale Island to Hardway. Over.'

'PCC. This is QHM. Permission to cross. Enjoy your paddle. Out.'

It was only a courtesy call, really. The Queen's Harbour Master had bigger fish to fry and much bigger vessels to worry about. Compared to cross-channel ferries and aircraft carriers, we were like mayflies on a pond. QHM was used to crazy night kayakers by now, but it was good to let anyone else who was listening know that we were around. We didn't want the naval police thinking that those low, slow-moving white lights belonged to insurgents sneaking up on the pride of the fleet.

I am always interested to see what ships are moored up around the naval dockyard: less and less each year it seems. There is a long naval history in our family. One of my ancestors was a navy captain back in Regency times and I've read the letters he sent home to his wife. The last one was written two hundred years ago to the day. It was a tough life out at sea in those days. I've often wondered what he would think if he could have seen Portsmouth as it is now.

As we crossed the harbour entrance, I felt a cold breeze blow but the water never stirred. I shivered and all at once every lights in the city went out and the harbour fell silent. There was a sailing ship moored up ahead: a tatty looking wooden vessel and I wondered if it might be a new exhibit for the historic dockyard museum.

A lone figure appeared on the foredeck and called out:

'Save us. I beg of you.'

'What's your problem, mate?' I shouted back.

'Cholera. One dead and many sick.'

My first thought was that we had stumbled into some kind of Napoleonic re-enactment, but the guy sounded deadly serious. He was either a brilliant actor or he really was in trouble. I did a first aid course a couple of years back but this particular scenario never came up for some reason, so I reached for the radio.

'QHM. This is PCC. Vessel moored between Gosport Marina and Burrow Island requesting assistance. Erm, they say they have a cholera outbreak. Over.'

There was a deathly silence. Not even the usual his of dead air. Then finally, a hesitant reply.

'PCC. This is QHM. Did you say "cholera"? What is the vessel's name? Over.'

Another gentle gust, warmer this time, blew across the harbour, breaking the still waters into myriad tiny waves. I turned around to see what the ship was called but there was nothing there. Just the bright lights of the marina and music drifting across the water from the bars and restaurants of Gunwharf Quay.

II – The Queen's Harbour Master

Extracts from QHM log 4th January 2016

15:00 - Work on the electrics in Semaphore Tower is over-running and it looks like we will be operating on standby power tonight. It's minus two outside, so here's hoping the heating works.

17:14 - Seven kayakers from Portsea Canoe Club checked in. Amazing what some people do for fun.

17:50 - Lights seem to have dimmed around the harbour. Hoping our contractors haven't managed to short out the substation this time.

17:58 – Kayaker reported unknown vessel moored off Burrow Island with medical emergency. Query cholera? Seven lights visible at stated location. There appears to be a ship nearby: possibly a three-masted sailing vessel.

18:02 – Lights are back on. No sign of sailing vessel, though PCC kayakers are still there. Called them and confirmed emergency services no longer required.

III – *The Captain*

Letter dated 4th January 1816

My Darling Maria

I do not know when, or if, this letter will ever reach you. After a difficult crossing, we arrived in Portsmouth this morning. Several of the crew were sick which I first attributed to the rough conditions. But when we reached the calm waters of the harbour, it was clear that they were beset with a fever which our surgeon believes to be the cholera.

We are now quarantined, and moored at the bitter-named Weevil Lake. The first of my crew died this afternoon and we laid his body out on Burrow Island: the only place where we are allowed ashore. The island is infested with rats, and so we covered his remains with earth and stone as best we could.

I feel myself now falling prey to the sickness and so you may consider what I now relate as nothing but a feverish dream, though I do not think it to be such.

As darkness fell, the wind dropped to less than a whisper and the sea was like a mirror. Men swore they could see their own reflections in its surface. It was as if there were two boats floating upon different sides of the same glassy film of water. I looked over towards the city and saw a strange vision. But if it were a vision of heaven, then it was not a heaven that any priest would recognise. I rather think of it as a window in time, a revelation of the future.

I saw the city illuminated by unearthly light and changed in almost every regard. There were wooden ships turned to iron, thousands of people parading along the waterfront in strange attire, and a white tower in the form of a great sail which loomed over it all.

Surely, I thought, the people who could build such wonders would be able to cure a simple fever? I cried out to them for help, knowing in my heart that they were too far away to hear. By a miracle, a voice answered from below and I looked down to see seven small boats, such as those used by the natives of icy artic lands. They asked what ailed me and I told them of our plight. One of their number spoke into the ether, calling for assistance and was answered by the distant voice of the Queen's Harbour Master.

For a moment hope rose in my heart and I dared believe we would be saved. But then wind blew in from the south in swirling gusts. A small wave, little more than a ripple, struck the bow. The mirror was broken and I looked up to find that we once again faced a dark city and a dark fate.

I take some comfort from my vision still. There are brighter times ahead: a future that our great-great-grandchildren may yet see. And if, one day, they should chance upon this letter then I ask of them this: one calm night, come to the place where our journey ended, take to the still dark water, and remember us.

The Spinnaker Tower

Rebecca Swarbrick

We must have seen that colour a million times before
Children squatting on a glass floor
Whilst Portsmouth spreads out below
Dressed all in blue
Their shoes jumble with reds, blacks and yellows
Stacked like a bonfire
Waiting to be set ablaze

(If you get us at that age you have us for life
And I thought it was just what I really liked)

One little girl finally decides to take control
Grabbing footwear by the buckles and shoe-laces
Hurling it through a gap in the tower wall

'What disregard for the tourists below' a mother mutters
Flattening out her uniform of red, white and gold
Forgetting to keep a firm grip on the ankles of her baby daughter
Sucked outside by the salty sea air.

Fragmented Self

Roz Ryszka-Onions

I follow her. She reminds me of my mum. She has that skittish, frightened look, you know? The look she had when postie brought the bills, the same look as when dad said 'I'm going to the pub' and mum never knew what state he'd be in when he got back. That look. Her eyes dart nervously from passenger to passenger. She picks at the zip of her handbag, which she holds like a baby in her lap, as if it's about to leap down and run away, as if she's protecting it.

The water is choppy and black. You can't see anything outside, just the lights coming from Portsea Island as we move away, and it is an island. People forget. It's so crammed full of schools, houses, churches, pubs, office blocks and people. I sit down next to her. I used to catch the Gosport ferry back home sometimes, before I passed. She can't see me, none of them can. I can make it so that they do. I can appear to be just like one of them but what's the point? I'm not and it's no use pretending otherwise.

I walk with her when she gets off. She walks fast but I can tell it's an effort. Age is catching up with her. I wish it would catch me, but even if I run as fast as the wind or crawl as slowly as a tortoise, age won't ever get out of bed to follow me. I want to go and see my mum, show myself, pretend she didn't lose me, pretend nothing happened. She'd say 'You've grown' and make my favourite, pasta bake and she'd try and hug me and find I wasn't really there. Not really.

People don't know this, but when a child dies, that child carries on growing. I say dies. I have to explain, I use death as a generic term. It covers, murder, coma, suicide, accidental, misadventure.

The result is the same. You die. It's too sad, so I don't go to see my mum. I want to all the time, but I never do. Today I trail up the High Street in front of the woman who reminds me of her instead. Just for fun I make myself visible and run on ahead and leap into the air. She startles but doesn't register me. The girl in the green parka with pink streaked hair. She's too busy dodging the local wildlife.

She's not to know this, but they're harmless enough. They look threatening in their hoodies, cigarettes dangling from their mouth as they swagger up the High Street. Can of energy drink for dinner and another cigarette, they stalk the corners waiting for their mates. Clusters of two or three of them walking aimlessly towards the waterfront. No, the danger lies not with them, but she doesn't know that. She doesn't know about the dark side, she just feels it. That's why she's afraid.

There she goes, she darts into the library. I don't go there. It hurts too much. I think myself into the café at Portsmouth and Southsea station. It tries to be shabby chic, finishes up just about plain dingy if you ask me, but I don't much care about décor, so I sit down at one of the corner tables and watch as an overweight man in an overcoat orders a black Americano and picks up a wrap. Apart from a down-and-out, who looks like he could be cool, nursing a mug of something, he's their only customer and it's kind of depressing, so I take a walk across the concourse.

There's little comfort for the dead. That's why I keep moving, you know? I sit on the train and go back and forth between here and Brighton, sometimes into Waterloo, but London is too big. I don't know it. I prefer home. When I see them, the pain I wanted to avoid, hits me. A girl, big boned with black, curly hair, her face scrubbed clean, in black blazer edged in red with the grammar school's gold crest on the pocket, is laughing with two boys at her side. They're smaller but I guess they'll catch up. Boys always do.

Her voice is preppy, clear as spring water. There's no cigarette rasp to it nor is it low with fatigue. I wonder where they live, in the big houses round Warblington or Old Bedhampton. I don't want to follow them. They'll have what I never had and can never have.

They're living the life I wanted. I passed my entrance exam to the grammar school. My teacher said I'd go far. I loved English, you know. Books. Literature. I was far ahead of my year but I never got to see that side of life. My mum, she tried, but we never had much.

My teacher, she was good to me, she brought me breakfast sometimes when there wasn't anything. She believed in me. Everyone needs someone to believe in them. I see her sometimes on the train. Not in town. I avoid the town during daylight. It's too cheerless to see everyone so downhearted when they're so alive. So blessed. So ignorant. But you'll be wondering what happened that I should have a golden, glittering future ahead of me and I should quite simply just die. Of course there was nothing simple about it.

But there's not much point me telling you. You won't believe me, I'll have to show you. I could take you through the city and show you the dead; they inhabit the place when you, the living, are asleep.

Some nights I go and sit in the Round Tower, look out at the black water ebbing and flowing like a heartbeat. I'm one of the few ghosts who go there. It's the sailor, he puts them off. He never got to say good-bye to his wife, he can't get over it, says he won't leave until she comes to him. He won't understand decades have passed and she's long gone. Night after night he sits in there waiting for her. He rants at anyone who goes near him, screams obscenities at them, but it doesn't bother me none. I sit down on the cold stone, which I can no longer feel, to stare out through the narrow fortress window and eventually he leaves me alone to my thoughts. I make up stories, you know. When I come here, it makes it easier. He's not here yet, it's so quiet. There's no-one here apart from the two teenage boys kissing by the water front in the dark. I don't know where the sailor goes during the day and early evening.

It's what I wanted to be, a writer. So, it's too miserable for me to go near a school or a library or a museum. I like the alleys, the sea, the back streets and the train ride. My story started near here.

I was eating a hot dog on Southsea Pier. My mum had a rare couple of quid spare. Me and Saanvi, we went together. She always had money, well, more than me. We wandered round the rides. It was summer, hot. We felt free, we were giggling. A man came up to us. He seemed nice. He offered us an ice cream. I said yes, Saanvi no. She said she'd buy me an ice cream, but he seemed so friendly. That's how it began. I met him after that. On my own. Once, twice, then he asked me if I'd do him a favour. At first I thought he was one of those paedos, so I turned to go, but he said *Hey, no, not like that. I'm looking for some boys and girls, you know poor ones, ones without mummies and daddies.* I asked him why. He said, *so I can look after them.*

That's how it started. I knew the kids he meant. The teachers weren't allowed to say, but we knew. They had that faraway look, you know the one a person gets when they're pretending it's not real, with their eyes glazed and their jaw hard, fists bunched. So I told him, I pointed them out to him. If I saw them sleeping rough or wandering, I called him on his special number. I took the train with him and I'd talk to the kids coming out of the other schools, then I'd tell him. I didn't understand why he kept hidden. If he was doing a good thing, why didn't he just go to the home, where they were staying and say he wanted to help out? He said, *people don't understand, Mish.* I heard the people in the homes are bad, that's what I heard, so I thought maybe that was why he didn't go to them.

He gave me money, he paid for my train rides and I loved the train and I loved to go in the car with him. Then I'd walk down to meet Saanvi and buy some floss for us to share, coz I had the money then. She'd ask me what happened, that we were so rich now and I said my dad got promoted. I wanted to be like her; her dad got promoted, and her mum too.

It was the best summer ever. We skipped onto the ferry and ran past the Round Tower, the Square Tower, all the way to the pier. I could pay for Saanvi's ticket now, not like before when she had to always pay for me. The breeze cooled us as we ran, getting in the way of everyone, a woman shouting out after us 'Watch where you're going, you idiots!', but she didn't sound angry, not like she would have done if it was raining. A woman pushing a buggy smiled at us. The sun on my face, my legs bare, no tights, no market puffa jacket, no howling wind and no rain like when I had to trudge home from school. We were so free.

Free for a while, coz no-one's ever really free. Not even ghosts. Summer was at an end, but we didn't really understand that, it felt as if it would go on forever. It was the last day of the holidays. As a special treat Saanvi's mum gave her five pounds and I had five pounds too. We were rich, as rich as the Queen. We bought floss, ice cream and a ride, tried to win on the 2p machines, but nothing doing. We were running away from the pier towards the East side of the island on the flat pavement, beside the shingle, as light as feathers in the cool mild sunlight. The blue sky and glittering water seemed never-ending, just like the summer.

Mish, Mish, I heard him call, as his car slowed. *Meet me here later, when it's dark,* he said. *I can't, I've got school tomorrow. What will I tell my mum?* He looked angry, the first time I ever saw him look like that. *You'll think of something,* he said.

We didn't run after that. Saanvi felt it too. It was as if the colour had bled out of the day and the energy out of our legs. We walked along the beach and picked out pebbles and shells that caught our eye. I kept one in my pocket to remind me of that summer. It was to be my last; it's as if I knew. It would have been my last year before Big School.

My mum made my favourite, pasta bake, but I couldn't eat it all. It wasn't the first time he'd asked me to meet him when it was dark. *What's the matter with you? Don't worry about school. You'll be fine. You've got Saanvi. You're still friends, aren't you?* I nodded, Saanvi wasn't the problem. I got ready for the next day and went to bed as soon as I could, sad, knowing I was lying to my mum. I waited until I knew she was asleep and then without waking my kid sister, Billy, I pulled on my leggings and my hoodie and grabbed my trainers. I shut the door behind me softly, waited to make sure no-one was awake, and ran.

I ran past the rows and rows of houses, through the streets, past the deserted shops, weaved my way through the boys in the hoodies who never sleep, dodged the men outside the Wellington, not stopping until I got to the ferry. The ticket man was concerned with the drunk swaying from side to side and the old woman with the bags kept him talking, so he didn't see me as I skipped on. Kids, we're small, invisible, if we're quiet. I crouched in the corner. No-one checks the tickets the other end and soon I was speeding past through the old town towards the pier where I was to meet him.

He was waiting. He didn't speak. I knew this was serious. I knew his secret, but I was too scared to tell. He was stealing children. *Don't mess up, Mish, I'm getting a good price for tonight. And you know I'll see you right.* He was nervous, I could tell.

Sometimes, when the stakes were high, he'd let on, like now, but most of the time, we played the game. He was helping the children without mummies and daddies. My job was to calm the kids down, so they came willingly. They were doped up, I could see that, but even so, they played up, sometimes.

He gave me a chocolate bar. *Keep your strength up.* We drove to Lock Lake, into a little alcove, where a boat was moored. *Go on, Mish.* I got out of the car, hopped onto the boat. The man, muscles bulging, his face red from windburn nodded at me, *Mish, watch yourself, they're a funny bunch.* I went below deck, went inside, the man with the red face close behind me There were ten, fifteen of them, skinny brown limbs, black wiry hair. An animal smell hung in the air, as the boys crouched in their cramped quarters. The one in the front row looked as if he was my age. He was rocking to and fro. I approached him. *It's all right. Come on.* I held out my hand.

The boy didn't take my hand but he stood up, swaying unsteadily from side to side. I held out my hand, but he didn't take it; he sort of folded in on himself and collapsed to his knees. One of the boys was sobbing. One started to be sick. The man with the muscles took up a bowl. *Here,* he said handing it to the boy. *Take the one at the back, he's the best of the bunch. He'll fetch a good price. The rest will be picked up in an hour.* I picked my way through the knot of limbs and held out my hand to the boy the man had pointed out. He took it. I led him upstairs and towards the car. We got in the back together. The boy wouldn't let go of my hand. I think he was younger than me. *Good work, Mish. He's a fine specimen.*

We drove, out of Portsmouth, onto the A27, to somewhere, it didn't take long. He stopped outside iron gates and they opened. We drove in, up to the front of the house. *Don't worry, I'll take you home soon, to your door.* He never came to my house, didn't want anyone to see him. This was taking so long. My mum would worry if she woke up. *Go on, go up to the door, lead him in, then come straight back.*

The door was huge and black, the windows were black. It was a mansion, with towers, surrounded by huge trees, sinister in the velvet dark of the night. The door opened a crack, and a wizened old face stared out at me. I heard the engine, I turned, but it was too late. He wheel screeched back down the drive. I ran after him. Stunned, the boy stayed on the doorstep. The gates shut. I leapt up them, started to climb. All I could think about was my mum. She would be heart broken. Who would help her with Billy? She would be alone. Billy was two years younger and still couldn't dress herself; she would never be able to do that.

Arms, strong arms grabbed me and pulled me away from the metal bars. Like flotsam, the man carried me inside. The door closed behind me and the boy turned to look at me. The wizened man in the grey suit smiled, his jaundiced eyes remained cold.

Next thing I remember, I'm standing next to my body, and the boy's body. His spirit was beside me.

Then the building shook and the very walls appeared to crumble. I glimpsed an angel. His wings were huge, powerful. As they moved together, then out, and in, and out, they created a wind. It felt like the breath of God, and a tunnel appeared. The boy turned to walk towards it. This time it was he who held out his hand to me. I shook my head. He went inside the tunnel and it disappeared.

I stood beside our two defunct bodies and watched as the wizened man did unspeakable things to them, things I won't repeat. I turned away before he had finished and thought myself back onto the ferry. There I could pretend that I was going home, back to my mum. I don't know how long I stayed there, going back and forth, back and forth.

I hid in a corner the whole night and when dawn arrived, grey and lacklustre I stayed on, going back and forth, back and forth. I don't know how long I spent there. Days, weeks, maybe months. Not thinking, not feeling. Numb. Dead. I thought of our kitchen and instantly I was there. My mum, her head buried in her hands. Billy, with chocolate smeared round her mouth, a pair of dirty socks on her feet, sitting in her knickers and vest at the table. The pain was so intense I couldn't cry. A silent scream escaped my mouth and I was back on the ferry, crouching in the corner. Back and forth, back and forth.

I suppose I wanted revenge, so a few times I followed him, but it made it worse, you know? I saw more and more misery, more and more children being taken, children whose mothers will mourn them through an everlasting veil of grief, a pain that no-one can ever take away, a pain that cripples like the worst killer disease there is. There is no such thing as a mother who doesn't care or a father who doesn't want to care. There are just tired, hopeless people. Sad, hurt, angry people.

The years cranked by and I wove new clothing each season. No need to buy it or wash it. No need to comb my hair or style it. I just think it. I'm a teen now. I alternate between blue and pink highlights. I saw Saanvi once and she was so full of life. A college girl, with her bag slung over her shoulder, her earpiece in, skipping down the steps, jaunting away from the station, through Havant. I go there sometimes to catch sight of her. I don't know why it doesn't hurt me to see her like it does the others. There's something about her, it takes the pain away.

So I dress like her now. Pink highlights, earpiece, leggings, green parka, nose piercing. From a distance you can't tell us apart. So you have it, that's my story. Oh hell, the sailor has arrived. Time to go.

The Guildhall. I love the lights in the square, the shadows they cast. I think that it's students' night at the Astoria. Here we are. It's packed, I can see the sweat rising in the air. The walls are steaming with it. They're so happy. Cheap beer sloshes over the edge of their plastic cups, laser lights flashing like pink lightning, the fire-eater in the cage limbo dances above the crowd. They dance, make-up slipping, their clothes sticking to their bodies. They're older than I'll ever be, yet the innocence shines in their faces.

There are layers in our society, secret layers, that can't be seen. To the side, in the concrete square tufted with grass, there's a manhole, an entrance into the other world. There's a labyrinth, a maze of corridors and airless, dark rooms, where they keep the children. As they dance and spill their beer, underneath their feet children dream; dream of running through grass barefoot, of standing in the rain, the water trickling down their faces, washing the dirt away.

They dream of bread, milk, rice, apples, a favourite blanket, a dog-eared book, a battered toy. These are the real undead, neither dead nor alive. I know them now, the trap doors, the side doors, the false walls hiding admission to their tortured world. There's no hope for them. I long to open the doors, let them go, but when I try to grasp the handle, or pull at the edges of the cover, my hand goes through as if through mist. I sit amongst a small group of teenage girls in the gardens. They're laughing, it must be cold, but they don't feel it, they're waiting for the boys to join them.

I'll never have a boyfriend. Saddened, I leave when they arrive. I sit on the ferry for a while. Back and forth, back and forth. Finally I catch the train to Havant, the last one of the night. I just made it. I'm the only passenger and I'm not real; it's just the driver and the guard. I get off, earpiece in, pretending I'm real. I walk past the man smoking in the alcove and the man leaning up against the wall. They can see me and it makes me happy to fool them this way. I wonder where the woman who reminds me of my mum is. She usually catches this train. It's usually me and her.

I start to jog towards the car park. I can see someone lying on the ground. Now I'm running, faster and faster. It's her car, the battered red Ford Fiesta. Her body is lying on the ground, blood leaking a burgundy stain onto the asphalt. I turn and she's standing behind me, watching her body spill its life force. She's crying.

I don't know how long we stand there together but eventually the tunnel appears behind her. She turns to look at it as it opens. She holds out her hand to me. She's so like my mum. I take it and we walk into the tunnel, together.

See How They Run

Susan Shipp

'That you, Dee?'

Al hooks his finger into the collar of his shirt above the knot of his tie, trying to loosen it. A squirm of unease rides down his overly warm back, and his throat constricts.

He stands still, listening.

Hearing nothing but the drumming of his heart, Al lets out a shaky breath and begins to move slowly down the frozen food aisle under the dimness of the overhead night-lights of the Sainsbury's that is within walking distance of his mum's house and The Royal Pub at the out of town end of Commercial Road.

He moves quietly, listening for the squeak of what sounded like rubber soles on the tiled floor. By the time he reaches the frozen peas at the end of the aisle, Al starts to suspect the only squeak he can hear is that caused by his own shoes.

Easing his neck from side-to-side, Al chides himself. *'You bloody, dinlo. They just be messin' with your head.'*

He smiles as the old Al resurfaces, and starts to strut down the aisle. Turning into the cereal aisle, he begins to whistle softly, continuing until he reaches the changing rooms where he stops to admire himself in one of the full-length mirrors.

His second month on the job as a security guard, Al thinks the black trousers, v-necked jumper and pale beige shirt make him look the business, although he's not sure about the burnt-orange coloured tie. Tugging it loose, he then tips his peaked cap back until it sits at a jaunty angle. Pulling back one side of his Day-glo padded coat to expose the walkie-talkie clipped to the wide black belt that hugs his slight paunch, Al grins. Turning side-ways, he sucks in his breath, and then pats his stomach, thinking *'Not bad, not bad at all'*. For a moment, the cockiness that saw him through his early teenage years springs back into his eyes.

Al, born Alfredo Raymond Packard in 1975, his name more to do with his mum's passion for Al Pacino than any Italian-American ancestry, is Portsmouth born and bred, raised in a time when people still knew their neighbours and didn't panic if kids came back with *scrazed* knees, or after dark. By the time he was fifteen Al, who had spent more time working on his dad's fruit and veg stall than going to school, thought he'd found his niche amid the hustle and bustle of market life. That was until his dad's fatal heart attack one busy Saturday afternoon whilst bagging up lemons, after which Al refused to work on the stall ever again. Drifting in and out of work, he eventually settled to the life of a hospital porter. Yet that too ended, which is why at the age of forty he is back home with his mum who, as much as he loves her, takes some living with.

*

The rattling wheels of a trolley banging through the warehouse doors cause Al to stop admiring himself. With a final check on his appearance he leaves the changing rooms and moves silently, following the babble of voices as the nightshift crew make their way to clock off.

Lagging slightly behind them, Dee, newly promoted to supervisor, searches in her handbag for her car keys.

Drawing level, Al coughs, and then rummaging in his coat pocket pulls out a packet of Polo mints. Slipping one into his mouth, he offers the roll to her.

She shakes her head. 'Nah. You're alroight.' Dee's Portsmouth accent is as strong as the perfume that almost conceals the smell of cigarette smoke clinging to her hair. 'Travis's done a sickie. Agency's sending someone. But you'll be on your own 'til he arrives and God knows when that'll be.'

Nodding, Al fights the urge to wrinkle his nose against the sourness of her breath. Sliding the roll back into his coat pocket, he smiles, and waits whilst she clocks out.

As she leaves, Dee stops and looks over her shoulder.

'I'm having a few of that lot round for a bit of a bash on Wednesday night.' She flicks her hand in the direction of the night crew. 'Nothing fancy, just a few beers and pizzas. Do you wanna come? You're not on the rota for that night.'

Al hesitates, and then shakes his head.

Since his illness it has taken him over twelve months to find employment, and now he has Al doesn't want to mess up. Doesn't want anyone bad mouthing him. Doesn't want anyone messing with his head.

As Dee makes her way across the car park, Al tightens his tie, and placing the cap on his head properly continues his rounds of the store. The dim light used for the nightshift stocking crew is gentle on his eyes, and now he is on his own Al feels a stillness come over him. Soft and still, like a moth in a cocoon.

As he rounds the end of Aisle 22 the lightness of a child's laugh coming from behind him turns his mouth dry, and the echo of tiny feet pattering on the floor makes his stomach clench. Even as he spins round, Al knows there should be nothing to see. Hopes there will be nothing to see.

Staring at the empty aisle, Al pulls on his ear lobe and then retraces his steps. He looks at his watch and a frown creases his face. The hands have stopped. Giving his wrist a shake, Al looks at the dial again. He puts the watch close to his ear. The strained tic-tic that makes the second hand judder is so faint, Al almost doesn't hear it. He taps the glass with his finger, and the second hand jerks back into life.

*

Leaving the quietness of the empty store, Al enters the staff room, almost recoiling at the stench of sour milk. From the open door he surveys the spray of biscuit crumbs, sweet wrappers, dried coffee-rings, and the half-used pint of milk left on the table. Al lifts the plastic bottle to his nose and takes a cautious sniff, even though the coolness of the liquid through the plastic already tells him it will be fine.

Using the wet sponge left on top of the mugs on the draining board, Al sweeps the detritus into the plastic waste bin. Placing the bin back by the sink, he rinses out the sponge, tucks it neatly behind the tap, and then squirts a liberal amount of air freshener around the room. It goes some way to disguising the puzzling smell of sour milk.

Pleased with his handiwork, Al puts the milk back in the fridge and takes out a can of Dr Pepper, on which he has written his name down the side in black felt-tip. Levering up the ring pull, Al sits on a plastic chair, places the can on the table and resets his watch using the staff room clock.

Dragging up another chair, he stretches out, placing his booted feet on the seat. Popping a couple of tablets from the bubble strip he'd slipped into the back pocket of his trousers before he left home, Al first jiggles them in the cup of his hand then tosses them into his mouth. Leaning back, he takes a long swig of Dr Pepper.

Resting the can against his chest, Al closes his eyes, waiting for the tablets to take away the edginess that has been building in him since the start of his shift.

*

The thin sound of a child singing 'three blind mice, three blind mice' jerks Al to his feet, the force of which sends the chair crashing to the floor. 'See how they run, see how they run...'

'Jesus!' The word bursts nervously into the empty room.

With his heart skittering at an alarming rate, Al creeps towards the staff room door. He hovers on the threshold, and then, gripping the edges of the doorframe, takes a deep breath, leans forwards, and dips his head into the corridor.

The dimmed night-lights prevent Al from seeing clearly to the end.

'Hello? Who's there?' The tremble in Al's whisper matches the acidic churning of his stomach. He raises his voice and calls out again. 'I know you're out there. So just quit with the messin'.'

Greeted by silence, Al's panic turns to anger.

'Have it your own way then, but when I gets hold of ya, I'm going to knock your bleedin' block off.'

The patter of tiny feet echoes down the confines of the corridor, and the lightness of a child's voice spills into the air once again.

'*They all ran after the farmer's wife, who cut of their tails with a carving knife....*'

The song fades, and although he can't see anyone Al hears the swish of the double swing doors and a soft thud as they close. He swallows hard. A tic begins to pulse beneath his eye.

Leaving the staff room, Al moves down the corridor, entering the store through the swing doors. They close with a dull thump. Walking from one end of the store to the other, turning down each aisle, checking out each nook and cranny, thinking of what he will do when he finds the culprit, he finds nothing.

With his heart easing a little, Al shakes his head, the frown returning to his pleasant features.

From his coat pocket, Al pulls out a pair of Poundland reading glasses. He perches them on the end of his nose, then takes out the strip of pills again.

Al nods at the writing on the reverse, satisfied he has brought the right ones. He taps the strip against the palm of his hand, a contemplative look on his face. Unlike the others, they give him a headache.

Returning them to his trouser pocket, Al massages the back of his neck with both hands, and then gently presses his thumbs against his eyes.

He mutters to himself as he makes his way towards the entrance of the store, twitching at every sound. Finally, irritated beyond patience, Al speaks out loud.

'Quit it, you bloody idiot.'

And, for a moment, he isn't sure if he's talking to himself or someone else.

*

The dimness of the store does little to ease Al's trepidation and, whilst completely at ease with his own company, he is beginning to wish Travis hadn't phoned in sick.

With a sigh, Al realises he has reached the front of the store. Darkness presses against the long glass panes rising from floor to ceiling. Street lamps splash light onto the perimeter of the car park, making the tarmac seem soft and malleable. And from Al's vantage point, behind the cold glass, the whole world looks soft, as if it could dissolve any second.

Al places his cap on the row of trolleys neatly stacked against the glass to his right, and then leans his forehead against the coolness of the night, waiting for the headache to subside. He closes his eyes.

*

It is some time before Al realises the streetlights have blinked out. Jerking his head away from the blackness that seeks to pass through the glass, Al fumbles for his cap.

His fingers touch the smooth sides of a wooden medicine trolley, the top of which, if closed, would slope like the desks he sat at in infant school. The top is open, revealing rows of neatly placed pill bottles, the labels facing towards him. Al blinks rapidly; a bead of sweat joins the nervous tic beneath his left eye. His cap is nowhere to be seen.

He steps back, then tentatively stretches out his hand to touch the medicine trolley, again. His trembling fingers slide through the honey glow of the wood until they touch the cold steel bars of a shopping trolley. Al moans. Fear curls in the pit of his stomach, as the medicine trolley fades before his eyes.

Something shifts inside him, a loosening of something already brittle. He begins to laugh. A high-pitched, girlish sound that struggles through the narrow airways of his chest, forcing its way past the tightness of his throat; it's a laugh that frightens him.

Staggering backwards, Al turns and runs. He pelts diagonally across the store, staggering at each twist and turn around the aisles, until he reaches the staff toilets. As he bangs through the door, he feels his bowels loosen. Stumbling into the toilet stall, Al fumbles with the belt on his trousers and then finally drops down onto the cold black seat. The relief is immediate.

Sat with his elbows on his knees, Al tries to ignore the alarming racing of his heart. Sweat runs down his face and the armpits of his shirt stick to him. Dragging his trousers back up to his knees, he fumbles in the back pocket for his pills. Popping a couple out, he tosses them into his mouth and swallows.

When his heart settles into a steadier rhythm, and his legs feel as if they can hold him, Al moves to the washbasin. Looking into the mirror, he sees a man whose eyes strive to hide the uncoiling of his sanity: a wash of sweat beads the greyness of his face, and his mouth is slack and trembling.

Pressing the knob on the soap dispenser, he begins to vigorously soap his hands. He rubs until they are coated white, and then holds them under the automatic tap. A trickle of cold water splashes down and then stops. The pipes cough and gurgle, then belch water onto Al's hands, until it comes out in a stinging torrent, washing the soap down the plughole in a foaming tide.

A laugh peals into the lemon-scented air. A woman's laugh that if Al heard whilst on a date would make him think his luck was in.

Another woman joins in. Their voices bang into each other. The sound of steel clattering against porcelain, combined with the stench of urine and other bodily wastes make Al grip the edge of the washbasin.

His stomach gives a dry heave.

Squeezing his eyes shut, Al listens to the high-pitched wheeze rattling from the tightness of his chest, and then risks another look in the mirror. Through clenched teeth he hisses in a breath that settles at the top of his lungs. His heart stops, relieving for a moment the constant drumming in his ears, then gallops into an unsteady rhythm.

Al stares at the gauzy image of nurses, dressed in pale blue uniforms with white collars and short sleeves ending in white cuffs. Their protective bibbed-aprons gleam under the yellow strip lighting. Small white hats are perched at the back of their heads, and their legs are hidden under black stockings.

His mouth dries, and for a moment the sluice room rolls away from his vision. It pops back with alarming clarity, revealing a starkness not alleviated by the dingy, cream-coloured wall and floor-tiles.

Al stares as a nurse pulls down the door of the hopper into which she places a bedpan. In one fluid movement she closes the door and stamps on the floor pedal to release a gush of hot water. Letting the circular door of the hopper fall towards her, she places the bedpan onto the steel drainer in readiness for scrubbing in the large butler sink, filled to the brim with disinfectant and bleach. As one nurse works the hopper, the other scrubs, and places the clean bedpans into the drying rack fixed to the wall. They giggle over the new doctor, whose twinkling grey eyes and soft Irish brogue are rumoured to have given him more than his share of one-night stands.

With a high-pitched yelp, Al runs from the staff toilet. He bangs his way into the staff room, and ignoring the ever-pervading stench of sour milk, slams the door shut. Dragging a chair from under the table, he wedges it against the door handle.

He leans over the sink and retches. The light dinner he consumed before starting his shift lurches upwards, splattering into the stainless steel bowl. Al retches until there is nothing left to leave his body. Turning on the tap, he cups cold water in his hands, rinses out his mouth, and then splashes water on his face, which he dries with a cotton tea towel.

Staggering back to the table, his legs feeling like rubber, Al sits down. Praying his shift is coming to an end, he looks up at the clock. His mouth gapes open at the framed floor plan of the Victorian built Royal Hospital hanging where the clock had been earlier.

The chair legs scrape across the floor as Al gets up and moves closer to take a better look. His head tells him it will be fine, but his gut tells him something quite different.

Perching his glasses on his nose, Al peers at the floor plan. Although the paper is yellowed with age, the writing is still clear enough to read. Running his finger over words protected by a thin pane of cracked glass, Al feels a chill run through him. As it ripples down into his legs, he snatches his finger from the glass.

'This is insane.' Al whispers the words, for to say them out loud, he thinks, will bring him to the brink, again.

But as much as his mind tries to find a way to refute what his eyes see, he cannot escape the fact that where he is standing right now, there had once been a children's ward, and a sluice room where the staff toilets are.

Either side of the floor plan are two framed black and white photographs, one showing the once imposing Victorian entrance of The Royal Hospital, the other, a long ward in which children lie or sit in neatly made beds or iron framed cots. Above each bed, Al can just about make out some of the pictorial nursery rhymes imprinted in the decorative frieze. At the far end of the ward stand two wooden rocking horses. In the foreground, matron, two nurses, and a doctor dressed in a white coat pose. They do not smile. The lighting of the photograph throws matron into shadow, but is clear enough to show the hem of her dress falls to the floor and the collar of her blouse is buttoned tightly against her slender neck.

Greyness begins to form at the corner of Al's right eye. As it darkens, a strong sense of foreboding tells him if he looks, and he so feels the need to look, it will be his undoing.

Lowering his gaze against the impossible, Al backs away until he feels the edge of the dining table against his bottom. Through quivering lips he takes a deep breath and looks up.

He feels the room waver, but forces himself to look at the dark shape of a woman, whose edges look as if they have been drawn with charcoal. A small child straddles her left hip.

The tumble of curls falling to the child's shoulders tells Al it is a girl. Her face has faded to grey, and her eyes stare blindly. With her thumb nestling in her mouth, she snuggles against the woman, whose skirt falls to the floor and whose blouse is high at her slender neck.

Removing her thumb from her mouth, the child's lips begin to move. Her voice is hollow and scratches against Al's torn nerves.

'... did you ever see such a thing in all your life, as three blind mice. Three blind mice, three blind mice, see how they run, see how they run...'

Al hears himself moan.

The woman moves with a serenity Al can only dream of, and at the door of the staff room stretches out an arm and passes through like liquid seeping through a crevice.

The lemon scent left in her wake can't quite hide the sour smell of sickness. It drifts, and then blinks out like an extinguished candle.

Wrapping his arms around his middle, Al begins to rock from side-to-side until, mercifully, darkness claims him.

*

The trolley's wheels squeak as it rattles along. Al can feel straps pulled tight across his chest, his thighs and his ankles. He struggles to raise his head, and then wishes he hadn't.

Two porters push the trolley, followed by a doctor dressed in a white coat. A scrawny, raven-haired nurse scurries alongside him, her shoes squeaking on the floor. The doctor whispers in her ear and the nurse smiles, a tiny dimple appearing in her chin. She is pretty in a hard sort of way, and her hair, neatly pinned back from her face, is covered at the back with a white nurse's hat. She smells of sickly sweet honeysuckle and cigarette smoke.

The trolley bangs through the double doors and Al squints against the brightness of the room. It smells of disinfectant and bleach. And it is cool, very cool.

Shivering, Al watches the nurse tie a surgical mask across her face. She moves behind him. Unable to turn his head without sending a searing pain into his brain, he listens to the sterilised instruments being placed on a metal tray and struggles to remember where he has seen her before.

As she moves back into his field of vision, Al tries to speak. His tongue feels too big for his mouth, and his words are muffled. He tries again, begging someone, anyone, to listen, to hear him. His voice sounds loud and frantic in his ears. He begins to struggle against the bonds binding him to the trolley. He begins to scream.

The scrawny nurse injects something into the drip inserted into the back of his hand. Al begins to drift. His eyelids droop and his words slur. He struggles to escape the darkness pulling him from the living world, into a stillness in which there is no sound save for the softness of his breath.

*

'Al, was doing so well.'

Doctor Howell speaks softly to Isla Packard, who tries unsuccessfully to find a comfortable spot on the hard plastic chair for her bony frame.

'But we cannot escape the facts. The CCTV footage shows Al in a state of extreme agitation, running through an empty store, and shouting at the unseen.' Doctor Howell allows his gaze to flicker away from the distrust in Isla's eyes.

With a sigh, he tries again, speaking slowly as if to a child. 'Isla. Al has clearly tried to self-medicate on a non-prescribed drug that he must have bought on the Internet.' Doctor Howell shakes his head. 'Whether the hallucinations are drug induced... I am unable to say at this time.'

Isla Packard focuses her eyes on the spot just above Doctor Howell's right ear. She does not allow herself the luxury of thinking, and his words roll over her to rest at a point where she can trap them behind a door she rarely opens.

Doctor Howell clears his throat. 'Isla?'

With a supreme effort she drags her mind away from the litany of Al Pacino films pattering in her head, and asks the only question she can think of. 'So what now?'

Doctor Howell purses his lips as if sucking on a straw, a frown drawing a line between his brows. He doesn't like the edginess in her eyes, but is slightly mollified by her smile.

'Al needs complete isolation. I can't say more until the detox is complete.' Doctor Howell stands and moves to the door. 'I'll let you know when you can visit.'

With a curt nod, Isla leaves the austere office. Once home, she draws the curtains, slips a DVD into the player, and, flopping down onto the leather sofa, waits for Al Pacino to wash the world away.

*

Al, dressed in long, white pants and a baggy white top, lies on a bed in a white room, where the lighting is low, and all outside sound is blocked. The restraints that prevent him from hurting himself don't cut into his flesh, yet they feel like steel bands.

He tries to shake off the drug-induced torpor that weighs down his limbs and blurs his mind. He keeps his eyes tightly closed. But, there is nothing he can do to block out the sound of a child yet not a child singing, its voice old beyond its years...

'... *Three blind mice, three blind mice,*
See how they run, see how they run,
They all ran after the farmer's wife,
Who cut of their tails, with a carving knife
Did you ever see such a thing in all your life,
As three blind mice...'

Tartarus

Joseph Matthew Pierce

Cosham, 1852

His suitcase held everything he owned. A couple of shirts, unironed and stuffed away in a rush. A photograph or two; anything he could salvage before he was collected just a few hours prior. The journey from London had not been kind. Storms had plagued their way. Now Alexander Danton found himself standing in the mud at the side of the road, in the company of a man he barely knew.

He should be along shortly' said Herman. He removed his pocket watch from his breast pocket. 'He is rarely tardy.'

Herman Messenger was a strange specimen, but Danton knew the sort well. He carried himself well, but with a gut that spilled out over his belt in every direction. His shoes were well polished, and he carried in his hand an umbrella that sheltered only himself from the rain. Mr Messenger, it struck Danton, was the kind of man not accustomed to making idle chatter.

'Do you know him personally?' Danton saw it appropriate to ask.

'I am acquainted' Herman replied nonchalantly. 'We have business in common, little more.' Upon noticing the cautious curiosity on Danton's face, he sighed loudly, as if the art of conversation pained him. 'They call him the Ferryman. These decrepit roads are his to roam. Though I cannot fault a man for holding an honest job, shipping poor souls into the Port's Mouth by land is a grim occupation.'

The mere mention of his destination chilled Danton to the bone.

Portsmouth, it was known, was a malodorous place; a haven for beggary, debasement, and drunkenness. The place was scarcely talked about in London's respected circles. There it represented little more than an underworld, far away from honest society.

In a wave of panic, Danton let his dignity give way.

'Sir, I beg of you. I do not belong in this place. You are held of high regard back in London. If you were to speak to...'

Danton was not permitted to finish. Herman Messenger spoke loud and clear without moving his eyes from the misty horizon.

'I do not pretend to know of the crimes that warrant your being here, Mr Danton, nor do I pretend to care. My job is to do His bidding. His word is my law. *Your* life is little more than my currency.'

'You cannot be so heartless?'

Herman sneered. 'Heart is an inappropriate burden in my line of work, Mr Danton. I am no judge. I am merely the messenger of my betters. Mine is not to reason why.'

Mine is just to do and die...

'I am sorry, Mr Danton, but there is nothing I can do. *His* word is final. Your fate is decided. You will live amongst the marshes or you will perish in its black waters.'

With that closing sentiment, Mr Messenger's eyes caught a glimpse of something through the fog. 'Here he is now. Your chariot awaits you, Sir.'

Through the dark and the rain there was a single glimmer of light that grew slowly brighter. Danton had to squint to see it at first, but soon the light became visible as the light from a lantern. The Ferryman, it seems, was never late.

A single horse drove the Hansom carriage. Its coat was so dark it was barely distinguishable from the barren countryside. The carriage was made from old wood, worn and aged. Its wheels were caked in mud and grime from its journeys. There was room for only one in this carriage. One single passenger, and the Ferryman.

The carriage always returns from that place empty, Danton had heard. He dared not imagine why.

The Hansom came to a slow stop on the dirt road before the two men. The reins that pulled about the horse's neck were held by a pair of fingerless gloves that seemed bloodied. Danton found his eyes transfixed. It soon became clear to him that he was petrified.

'Long night, Charon?' Mr Messenger called up to the Ferryman.

'Aye, that it is' replied Charon. His voice was harsh and foreboding. 'Another for the fire?' He spoke now directly to Danton. 'What have you done, I wonder?'

Danton could feel the eyes of the Ferryman look him up and down. Once again he felt the burden of guilt on his shoulders. *He knows,* he thought to himself.

'For St James's?' asked the Ferryman.

'No, no' answered Mr Messenger, 'There is a special place for this one. *He* wants him taken to Somers himself.'

The Ferryman adjusted the filthy cap upon his brow. He looked again to Danton and raised an eyebrow. There was almost pity in his eyes. 'So be it' he said, stifling a fit of coughs. 'In you get, *boy.*'

Danton took no offence at the slur upon his age. When he left London he was barely into his third decade. Too young, some would say. *But I will never see the wisdom of age*, he thought. *Not where I am going.*

Mr Messenger's umbrella was held up to the carriage to allow Danton to take his seat. The gesture was a civility only; one last gesticulation of good will. Or perhaps it was a condolence. Regardless, Herman Messenger never intended to set foot onto the Ferryman's carriage. His job was now concluded. His escort had gotten him as far as the end of the mainland. The road into the Port's Mouth belonged to the Ferryman and the Ferryman only.

'You have been dealt a poor hand, Mr Danton' said Herman with another sigh. 'That much is obvious to me. But here I would advise you take caution. Abandon your presumed superiority and quieten your tongue, lest the towns of Portsea Island claim you as their own.' And with a single tip of his hat, the Messenger disappeared from Danton's view.

Messenger exchanged a few civil words with the driver, inaudible against the harshness of the rain, before the reins were whipped and the carriage began its journey south.

The Ferryman's carriage trundled down the old dirt road and passed little in the way of other traffic. It became immediately clear to Danton that any vestige of civilisation had long since been left behind him. What lay ahead for him through the rain and fog was left to his treacherous imagination. He knew that his destination lay somewhere on Portsea Island; an island of prosperous docklands, filthy slum towns, and unforgiving marshlands. Beyond that, Danton could only guess what lay ahead for him.

He dared not attempt conversation with the Ferryman. He was assured that anything he could say would lead to his nerves getting the better of him. So he simply let much of the journey pass with only the harsh whisper of the wind for company. It gave him the time to gather his thoughts and accustom himself to the quickly chilling air. Though he could not see further than ten feet into the distance, the coast was clearly approaching. He could hear it as the carriage passed over a bridge of mud and grime. To either side the road sloped down into still waters. Danton wondered how many got lost in this desolate land.

The Ferryman knows the way forward.

Placing his suitcase upon the floor of the Hansom, Danton grasped onto the armrest and peered out into the night. Curiosity had gotten the better of him. The gas lanterns gleamed so enticingly, they had entranced him from his seat.

The mud gave way to dirt with each passing light. The paved roads of London seemed now such a luxurious commodity. Here, the wheels of the Ferryman's carriage seemed to slide effortlessly across the river of wet soil. It was as if the carriage barely touched the ground at all.

From the darkness houses grew. They were little more than shacks, crudely held together with vague remnants of plaster and sediment. Rain poured from rudimentary drainpipes, joining the sordid pools that gathered on the roadside. Yet, Danton saw no people.

'I say, Ferryman?' Danton called up to his company. 'Are these dwellings occupied?'

The voice of Charon rippled through the carriage, old and deep. 'Yes.'

'By whom?'

There was a momentary silence before Charon spoke again. 'The lucky ones.'

For some time, Danton did nothing but pick at the holes in his leather gloves. His clothes were wet through, his trousers caked in mud, and he struggled to understand whether it was the cold or fear that made him shake so.

He knew nothing of his destination but a single name. *Somerstown*. It was scrawled onto the piece of paper that was forced upon him on his hasty exit from the metropolis. It seemed so long ago now.

My Paradise Lost...

Danton's eyes were drawn once again to the thick gloom in the air. The slums that surrounded him did not bode well for his destination. The houses seemed to be growing older with every passing street. Even worse, he could feel eyes upon him. The carriage was being watched.

'Ferryman?' Danton called to his guide. 'What do they call this place?'

'Buckland' he answered.

Buckland. 'Is Somerstown much like this?'

'No.'

'I should hope not...'

'These are old towns' the Ferryman interjected. He spoke in a deep and songlike tone.

'Buckland, Landsport, Fratton, they existed well before the city, well before the roads joined them. Now the Port's mouth is slowly engulfing them. One by one. Soon everything that was natural about this place will be taken by the greed of man.'

The greed of Man? Or did he mean a particular man?

'And what of Somerstown?' he asked curiously. 'Is it as old as the rest?'

'No' the Ferryman answered certainly. 'Somerstown is new... Somerstown is *his*.'

The tone of the Ferryman's voice was not providing the comfort he desired. He returned to his seat, trembling and apprehensive about what lay in store for him further south. 'I cannot fathom what...'

Danton was cut short when he was jerked from his seat. It took him a moment to comprehend what was happening, but it soon became clear that he was no longer alone in the carriage. A filthy, lacerated hand was manically grasping over the armrest until it reached Danton's coat sleeve. It tugged for a moment before Danton managed to swat it away. As it left the carriage, the hand found the handle to Danton's suitcase. It was swiped away into the darkness.

'Stop!' Danton called after him. 'Thief!'

He swung open the crude door of the Hansom carriage and leapt out into the unknown. His shoes were immediately engulfed by thick mud up to his ankles. The thief, he soon found, was quickly disappearing into the night.

'Stop!'

It took all of his considerable effort to move in the thick grime. For every step he took, his shoes seemed to sink deeper. Between each heaving exertion he glanced up to find the thief further away until he vanished completely into the rain. Danton called out one last time, but he was met with nothing but darkness. His heart sank.

I am penniless in this cesspool, he thought hopelessly. God help me now.

'Ferryman' Danton spoke quietly, 'I have been robbed.'

When he turned, he found the carriage was nowhere to be seen.

'Ferryman?' Panic began to take him. He swivelled upon the spot. 'Charon? This is no time for trickery! Ferryman!'

The longer he remained in this thick sludge, the more of his willpower was sapped from him. It was then that he saw the figures emerge.

There was one at first; a vague silhouette against the darkness. But then there was another, and another. Soon, there were figures from every direction. Danton dared not call to them, lest his presence be announced, though he feared his protests had already done that.

Then a hand grasped at his shoulder.

He spun round and was met with the black eyes of a man. He wore a cap upon his head, and his hair was stuck to the side of his cheek. The very touch of him chilled Danton through and through. He was weak, and he was vulnerable. He could not say a word.

As quickly as he had found himself in the mud, he was pulled from it.

'This man has nothing worth your time, *vagrant*,' came a voice. It was coarse, yet comforting. 'Leave the streets. You shall never poach upon the Ferryman's path.'

As if compelled by some unexplainable fear, the black eyed man stumbled backwards before turning heel. Danton watched as he retreated into the fog from whence he came, back into the darkness of the urban landscape.

Danton turned to his saviour, and found him unlike what he expected. The Ferryman, he found, was nowhere in sight. Instead, there stood a man, sixty years in the face, but built like a man in his prime. He wore the suit of a gentleman, not at all unlike those favoured back in London. In fact, if Danton was not conscious of his situation, he would have easily mistaken him for a metropolitan man. His suit was dirty, however, and sodden in the rain.

'That damned man took my bag!' Danton lamented. 'Damn and blast this accursed place!'

The old man merely smiled. 'Many have, dear boy. You would not be the first.'

Brushing himself off, Danton straightened his back and traipsed forward through the sludge towards his saviour. 'You,' he said, 'What do they call you?'

The man raised an eyebrow. 'Me? They call me many things.

Lord... master. But you may call me Somers.'

'Somers?' Danton questioned. 'Haydn Somers?' When the man nodded, he recoiled. 'You are not at all what I expected.'

'Appearances are but the surface of character' the man replied. 'And who, may I ask, are you?'

Danton fished about in his pocket and removed an envelope. Within was authorisation of passage into the Port's Mouth. 'I was told to find you at this address.'

Haydn Somers received the letter and glanced over it for a moment. His eyes began to deform at the passing of every sentence. Danton himself had not read a word, but he could guess as to its contents.

'Alexander Danton' Somers said. He pursed his lips as if he savoured the very name. 'Welcome to the island of Portsea. Come...' He beckoned Danton to his side, '... let me show you your new home.'

*

With the owner of the land by his side, Danton's nerves were calmed somewhat. He did wonder for a time how Mr Somers had the courage to wander these streets at night, especially in weather such as this. He seemed to have some physical authority over the residents of this place. Danton felt safer in his company.

'You should know not to leave the Ferryman's carriage' Somers said as they walked. 'This city is dangerous to those unaccustomed to it.'

Danton could not help but agree. 'Indeed. I have only been on this cursed island for half an hour and I am now poorer than the vagrant that pocketed my purse. First impressions of this place are poor to say the least.'

'Oh?' Somers acted surprised. 'And I suppose that dearest London is completely lacking of thieves and vagrants?' He chuckled to himself. 'This is old land, Mr Danton, very old land. It may not be an old city, like London, but it is old land. The Port's Mouth is growing accustomed to its urbanity. The villages on this island are finding their feet in the age of sprawling cities in any way they can. Its' people, they too must adapt to the ages.'

'By thieving from visitors?'

Somers narrowed his eyes at the slight. 'If they must.'

In the company of Haydn Somers, Danton was led further into the island of Portsea and into the place he called Somerstown. The bleak scenery that surrounded them confused him. The urban began to creep higher with each passing street. The vague hints of cobblestones formed underfoot, though it was patchy and uneven. This place bore the likeness of a newly constructed townscape, quite unlike the villages they had journeyed through.

'The Port's Mouth,' the landowner began, 'was once little more than its namesake. It was a port, fuelling the empire with fresh souls to extinguish on foreign shores. Battlements were raised up to protect this place from all that may wish to take it; and yet it wasn't enough. The island was little more than an ill-used marshland.'

Somers chuckled. 'The allure was strategic only. I mean, what use is land so sodden and devoid of hard soil?' His mouth slowly lost its grin and he gazed out into the wilderness before him with contemplative eyes. 'This land was my father's, and his father's before him, and so on and so forth. However, they failed to see the potential of such a place. I saw this land for what it was: opportunity. Roads can be laid. Marshes can be drained. Nature, it seems, can be tamed.'

Through the rain, Danton could hear commotion. There were voices in the distance, and they were moaning.

'What is that noise?' he wondered aloud.

'The townspeople, I imagine' Somers said as he turned a corner. 'Not unlike you, once upon a time.'

Around the corner, the road opened up to accommodate the courtyard of a house rather unlike anything Danton had ever seen. It was visible through the rain as a gothic manor. Fences encased its grey bricks like a rusting cage. Gargoyles guarded its entrance. Harpies and all manner of creatures stood vigil over the outer courtyard. This, it was abundantly clear, was the manor of Haydn

Somers.

The iron fences reached for the blackened skies like vines up a wall, and just before them was the source of the commotion. There was a crowd, perhaps three dozen in total, clamouring towards the iron bars, reaching into the manor's grounds with bizarre desperation. It was an unnerving sight, which only grew worse.

With his hands clasped behind his back, the owner of the land strolled towards the crowds. Danton went to advise against it, but was shushed before he could do so.

'I have nothing to fear from these people' Somers said as they reached the crowd. 'They know their Lord.'

The first of the crowd noticed their approach. More heads began to turn and soon the entire crowd's eyes were upon them. The moaning ceased, as did the clamouring. All attention turned to Somers and Danton.

Though this unnerved Danton incredibly, Somers seemed not at all perturbed. The crowd, in an extraordinary occurrence, parted to make way for him. An aisle was created leading toward the main gate, down which Somers marched. Danton could only follow, though he did so with unease. These people, he noticed, were not at all well. He saw all manner of ailments - pox, warts, blotches, bruises cuts; all the scars of a hard and malnourished life. Danton felt anxious in their presence.

The eyes of the crowd were not on him, however. They were upon Haydn Somers. The lord of the land approached the gate as an idol of complete adoration. It was only once the great iron gates swung open and they entered the property that the spell broke, and the desperate nature of the crowd returned to them. Danton skipped backwards as the crowds began to mass once more, but not one of them stepped foot into the courtyard. The iron gate resumed its vigil.

'They want to get in' Danton said as they advanced through the courtyard. It seemed empty; devoid of anything living. Any tree that may have once stood in this garden had long since wilted and died. All that remained were empty flowerbeds and fountains long dry.

'Are you a philanthropist?'

'In my own way, yes' Somers agreed. 'I take under my wing those that the metropolis casts out. They flock here, some by their own accord. And some, like you, have no choice in the matter.'

'They seemed desperate to enter your manor.'

The lord of the land sighed. 'Out there, they know nothing but scarcity and pauperism. This manor is known to be a haven for abundance. This is where the rich take shelter.'

'I can see why they would be so eager.'

Haydn Somers did not seem to agree. 'They are *deluded*.'

The doors of the manor opened before Somers and his guest, and immediately the stench engulfed them. Danton was so taken aback that he reached into his coat pocket and placed a handkerchief to his nose and mouth.

A putrid hallway stretched out before them. It was narrow, damp, and decrepit. The rafters above his head creaked and dripped, whilst those beneath his feet buckled and sank under every step. And there were people there. In the halls they littered the floors like squatters. Their eyes were glazed and transfixed on their masters as he strolled past.

Out of the hallway there grew numerous rooms. Their doors were open wide, and their contents easily noticeable to Danton's inquisitive eye. In one, he could see tables upon tables of food; rancid and rotting. The tables swarmed with maggots, and yet there were people sat at them. They ate with their hands, not pausing for breath, weeping as if they had no choice in their gluttony. In another, vast betting tables were set up. The guests circled about, wallets filled with every decreasing amounts of coin. In the next, Danton could barely see through the steam. But inside he could see the naked forms of two dozen guests, lustrous and unceasing.

This is the home of everything sacrilegious...

Danton found himself confused. 'This is where the rich take shelter?'

'Does it disturb you?' Lord Somers asked as they made their way towards the back of the manor.

'Yes' Danton agreed wholeheartedly. 'It is most awful to behold.' Somers placed his hand to Danton's back and smiled. 'You pity them, do you?'

'Most definitely' said Danton. 'It is a repulsive way to live.'

'It certainly is' Somers said as he ushered Danton towards the end of the hallway. 'I am so glad you agree.'

Through the final door, Danton was met with the open air once more, and another courtyard. A thin wooden rail ran around white decking, painted white. It was bright, Danton found, and it was only then that he felt the absence of the rain and peered up at the sky. Where it was just moments ago foreboding in its wrath, the morning sun had begun to peer through in the far distance. Though the evening fog was still thick, beyond the channel, Danton could see into the distance. And what he saw chilled him to the very bone.

He could see an ocean, dark and troubled. The vague hint of better lands could be seen beyond its waves- steeples and lights were distinguishable through the lessening fog. But that was all it was.

A far off Elysium...

The courtyard overlooked a marsh that stretched out beyond the borders of Somers' estate and out in either direction. But it was not the marsh that concerned Danton so. It was the people who were traipsing through it.

Haydn Somers relished the expression on Danton's face. He seemed to thrive on the shock of it all. 'Wonderful, is it not? The boons of convict labour?'

He drew Danton's attention to the West, and to the built up land beyond the marsh. In sight there was a dockland. Battlements encased it in an archaic belt that overflowed with the gluttony of its urbanity.

'They arrive from the sea' Somers continued. 'The Port's Mouth welcomes them, and I take them in. Here they live the consequences of their actions and serve their labours.'

Danton was repulsed by what he was witnessing. There was a single endless line of poor souls, shepherded from the Port's Mouth, through the marshland, and into the heart of Portsea Island.

'Do not look so shocked, *boy*' said Somers with a smirk. 'This is enterprise at its finest.'

'This is not enterprise,' said Danton, 'This is slavery.'

'That is the way of the world!' Somers exclaimed. 'Every great city is built upon the foundation of slavery. Rome was moulded by the sweat of bondage. Paris stands upon tunnels of bone and marrow. Your own beloved London is built on the remains of the Celt and the Saxon. Cities cannot be built without blood and toil- without the destitute to support them.'

Danton took a step back. Somers remained by the railing. He seemed to grow taller with every word.

'There are two types of men in this world, Danton' he continued. 'There are those who build empires, and those who provide its foundations. Vagrancy is a plague upon humanity- and obstruction to progress. *I* am a man of progress. I have built my empire. My name will be immortalised in the annals of history.'

'But you, what are you, Danton? You are no vagrant. No, you are something worse. Decadent. You lived like a king in your depravity; selfish in your abundance and merciless in your greed. So confident were you in your own merit that you could not so much as fathom that you may every fall from such grace.' Somers now rose up so that he blocked out of the remnants of light in the sky. What remained was a black silhouette against the gathering clouds. 'You thought yourself answerable to nobody. You thought your wealth would save you from the underworlds beneath you. No. Every action is answerable. Every debauchery has its consequence.'

In the shadow of the lord of the land, Danton shrunk. He faced judgement and he could think of no way to defend himself. Every accusation thrown his way rang true. Danton knew it in his heart, and felt nothing but regret. It all seemed a lifetime ago now.

'I think you have me mistaken...' Danton began.

Somers turned violently. 'I am never mistaken! Here, I am sovereign. I built this land from nothing. I know it. I *understand* it. Every port, every road, every forsaken marsh. And I know those who dwell here.' The owner of the manor drew slowly closer. 'What is it that puts you above them?' Somers asked. 'Is it the coin in your pocket? The stitching on your coat?'

At that moment, the doors to the manor began to shiver on their hinges. Something inside was trying to break through.

'Perhaps it is your posture? The dialect of your speech? Perhaps it is simply years of being told so that made you the better of everyone else!'

'Mr Somers, I...'

Somers ignored him. 'Strip away the lapels, the cufflinks and the polish, and what is left but everything that such material decadence created. Pride. Greed. Lust.' Somers sneered as the rumbling from the doors grew more severe. 'Here your sins are brought to light, Alexander Danton, and they are many. Here, I am sovereign. Here, you are *nothing*.'

The doors burst open to the sound of a dozen lost souls hitting the decking. They clamoured to their feet, their eyes glowing in the twilight. They were transfixed on Danton. It scared him from his sure footing.

'You do well to be frightened' said Somers calmly. 'These are your family now.'

'No!' Danton said. He swatted away his host as he backed away against the railing. 'No, I do not belong here. You have me wrong. I am not like these people.'

When he could back away no further, he took a glance over and out into the great marsh that stretched out to the sea. There truly was nowhere to go.

'Mr Somers, please...'

'My dark city is being built on the bones of men just like you, Mr Danton. It will stand as a monument to the sins of better men. This is not a place for the disgraced, nor the damned. It is an honest reflection; the other side of a coin, nothing more.'

Somers was now so close that Danton had to arch his neck away.

'Welcome to the underworld that man created. Welcome to all that your decadence wrought.'

Danton could do nothing else but swat the madman away. In the face of Haydn Somers and the horde of possessed paupers massing behind him, Danton threw himself over the railing and down into the forsaken marsh. He sunk deep into the mire, but still managed to bring himself to scramble to his feet and press forward.

With the vast expanse of desolate marshland ahead of him, Danton quickly lost his way. The manor of Haydn Somers lay behind him, but ahead the thick grime only grew deeper. The waters crept ever higher, until the filthy grime lapped up around his waist. Every movement sapped at his willpower until he could scarcely move any further. It was only then that he decided to stop and rest a moment.

Only for a moment. Only for a moment...

As he sank ever lower, Danton took a last glance back at the manor of Haydn Somers. It stood at the edges of his new dark city, where the sins of the urban masses lay their foundations upon the smothered villages of this ancient land mass. It was then that Danton understood. This was never the end of the world. It was merely a city built upon the sins of men like him.

The sins of the civilised world manifest...

A hand reached from the marsh and wrapped its skeletal fingers around Danton's wrist. Two more found their ways around each ankle. Danton offered no resistance in the end, even as his predecessors dragged him to the deepest depths of the marsh. He found his place at the side of hundreds just like himself. Lost souls brought to nothing in this place.

Welcome to the underworld that man created...

My Dark City...

On the Wharves

Tom Millman

If there was one thing Lydia hated it was spring. Even as it grew brighter, the days longer, things that should still be sleeping, awoke. The moon painted the streets of Portsea with the twilight, giving the buildings an eerie glaze. In the distance she could hear the drunken callings of the vagrants who made the wharf their home.

Forcing her collar up, Lydia brushed an auburn strand from her eyes and replaced her tricorn hat. She tensed as something clattered in an alley nearby. As she approached, her hand on the hilt of the falchion, she sighed as she heard discontented mewling.

Lydia ducked into the alley as she saw two Redcoats approaching her, Brown Bess muskets resting against their shoulders, the bayonets catching the light. Those wigs looked ridiculous but who was she to say what was fashionable.

'You heard about the Americas?' The first said.

'You mean that the French are helping out the Patriots?'

The other nodded before berating the other about how the French shouldn't get involved and that it wasn't right, not after that revolution. Served them right though. Lydia agreed they had no right to get involved.

Lydia glanced around, trying to find the Grimm Bell. Removing her spyglass she spied it in the north. While being a portal Grimm Bells were bloody inconvenient to find. Why she had to come on the solstice night she didn't know. The message she was given was clear but there had been no sender. What use were seagulls if they don't know who sent them? 'Come to the bell on the peal of midnight and all will be revealed.' Why the damn Folk have to be so cryptic she would never know.

Lydia thought herself fit but these cobbled streets were a pain. Her effort rewarded her however and she caught a glimpse of what she had been searching for. The Grimm Bell eerily refracted the moonlight as Lydia reached it. The humans called it the Muster Bell. The guards might not like the fact she had snuck into the Dockyard. Oh well. Lydia had found it too easy to sneak in. These blasted Redcoats were lazy. On the pillar, there were three hooks poking from the pole. She wondered what the doctor would have made of that, he was focused on pointing out dangerous circumstances and objects.

Rifling within her pockets she brought out a black box with musical signs engraved onto the wood. Lydia's hand formed around the three bells, drawing them out. The bells sounded the notes C, E and G. With a little tinkle she worked out which one was which. These bells were old and had lost their embellishment, and Lydia had damn trouble remembering which one she needed to start with. She hooked the bells in ascending order starting from the bottom hook.

Lydia put them in the right order, or at least the order that she thought they should be in. From inside her cloak she pulled out a little hammer, and tapped each in ascending order. The bells did their duty and chimed. Lydia swore in happiness. She would have liked to see Mad King George beat that. In his case he would have probably thought he'd imagined it.

Two lines of light sprouted from the highest bell and outlined a door. Taking a deep breath, Lydia put one hand to the doorknob, twisted and sighed in relief. This was the right door, thank God. Lydia still feared that ebony door would appear. The things that lurked behind it, she never wanted to experience again.

'Mistress Lydia, a pleasure to see you as always.'

The speaker was a robust man, the Innkeeper; his greasy hand patted his scum ridden apron. He always gave her a bow, but something in his eyes raised her hackles. The common room was packed for the beginning of the Spirit Festival, all sorts of odd Folk around.

The man turned to a table, grabbing a purse filled with salt.

'Mistress, if you could present your sword?'

Lydia unsheathed the falchion from the back scabbard and held the blade horizontally towards him. The man's hands shook as he poured an unsteady stream of salt, which formed a line on her blade, some of the salt gracing her shoes.

With a practiced motion, she kept the blade horizontal, pivoting towards the door. Lydia swiped her blade into an arc, the salt penetrating the floor and air, an old and stupid superstition. If anything was pursuing her, her sword would fare her better than salt but niceties had to be observed.

Being a Hemlock meant she was the equilibrium, the balancer for the Folk. Lydia damned the doctor each new day for dragging her into this. Each encounter with the denizens left her with a new scar. Lydia bunched her right fist. It felt wrong. Her ring, where had it gone?

The Folk who had gathered here were from all across the known world. The Orchid Sect loomed in the corner with their katanas at their sides ready to be drawn. There was a Frenchman around one of the ale slopped tables having a disagreement about metallurgy with one of his comrades. Lydia wanted to spit; the French should never have interfered. The only upside was watching them wear those stupid embroidered breeches.

Innkeeper motioned her to pass but she did not move. Lydia knew fear, she had seen it in other's eyes and she had felt it in her own; the Innkeeper was terrified.

'What are you scared of?'

The Innkeeper cowered then motioned her to a table. One of the maids by the bar nodded and drew two flagons of ale. She swayed her hips as she passed a ruffian; perhaps that's the sort of man she liked. Lydia pulled her sleeve to cover her hand, a white line apparent on her middle finger. She hissed in distaste as ale slopped over her fingers. She had never liked the smell of ale; the drunkards who commonly harassed her stank of it. No a refined lady, Lydia thought, would drink only the finest vintages. But being a wharf rat didn't pay well and ale was the only drink on this menu.

'You know me, mistress, I'm not one to be spreading tales but my little Madeline has gone missing, see.'

Whatever Lydia had expected it was not this. 'When did this happen, Innkeeper?'

'Three days ago, but it wasn't just my Madeline. Several little'uns have disappeared.'

Surprised, Lydia comforted Innkeeper, stroking his arm gently. A whistle broke the somewhat tender moment as her friend appeared from the Orchid Sect.

'I'll find her Innkeeper; I'll find her and bring her back to you.' Lydia made her pleasantries before leaving.

A severe face met her own, one that had so often been graced with a smile and laugh, a smile that had often comforted her.

'Ayaka, what are you doing here?' The young woman had her hand poised on her katana as Lydia approached.

'You know very well why I am here. Where is it?' Lydia tensed, not only with confusion but with terror.

'I don't know what you mean. What do you think I have taken?'

Ayaka looked around to make sure that none of the patrons were able to hear them. 'The Twinleaf flute.'

'That old stick? What makes you think that I would even want it, let alone steal it?'

Something rebounded off Lydia's chest, a ring with an engraved crow, the symbol of her profession.

'My ring. Where did you find it?' Lydia tried to recall when she had last seen it.

Something in her memory tugged at her, a soothing tune, and an enchanting tune.

'It was in the sanctuary, on the floor near the pedestal that bore the flute.'

'I haven't been to the sanctuary since last summer. Someone must have planted it; you know that I wouldn't do that, Ayaka. You know me.'

Something softened in Ayaka's expression, but then immediately hardened. The accusation in her eyes hurt Lydia. She knew why but she didn't want to admit it.

'Lydia, you have twenty four hours to return the flute or else.'

'Damn you Ayaka, you know I didn't do this. Let's team up - you and me. We can find it together.' Lydia put a hand towards her friend.

'This action is irrevocable; whatever was between us is gone now. A word of advice, Lydia. If you want to survive this, return the flute, or you'll regret it.' Ayaka clasped Lydia's hand before turning away leaving a flower in her hand. An orchid. The blasted Folk are risking invoking the Orchid Protocol.

Lydia surveyed the patrons, looking for Ayaka in the inn but there was no sign of her. Shoving patrons aside and kicking chairs she grabbed hold of Innkeeper's arm.

'Where is Obake?'

XXI

Lydia traced the figure's path through the crowd. A man of middling years, wearing a tricorn cap similar to her own but while her coat was well cared for, his was patchy and dripping wet.

Running on rooftops was a hobby for some but to Lydia it was blasted inconvenient. Her target was making their way up West Street towards the channel. Why was he going to West Street, there wasn't a Grimm Bell anywhere near there? So whatever he was doing he wasn't running away.

Most pursuers think crowds are an inconvenience but Lydia knew it was the best way to slow someone down. Vaulting to a smaller rooftop, she dodged out the way of a guard. Lydia never understood why they wore those wigs. Why would they want to look older?

To her left, the two buildings were close enough that she could ease herself down. Lydia slipped in and out of the crowd before she got ahead of him. The fool walked too close to the alleyway she was hiding in. She was the Venus flytrap and he her prey.

She braced herself as she threw him up against the wall.

'Mistress Lydia, what a pleasure' he whispered, hesitant to brush his throat against her dagger.

'Surprised to see me, Obake? I personally don't like your new look. Why not show me that face I love so much?'

Lydia pressed the dagger, causing a pinprick of blood to trail down his throat. The man's face spasmed, shaking uncontrollably, the features melting away until only the mouth and ears remained.

'There we are. You weren't expecting to see me, were you?'

'The... the Orchid Sect put the word out.'

Lydia tightened her grip on the dagger. 'Yes, that I stole the Twinleaf flute... but you know I didn't do it, don't you, Obake?'

Obake's facelessness unsettled her even now, but she had to keep her focus. He nodded, the edges of his smile stretching.

'Now tell me Obake, who did take the flute?'

Obake shook his head. 'I can't say. Please don't make me say. He'll kill me.'

Lydia pressed her advantage. 'What makes you think that I won't kill you?'

His gulp was audible. 'They say he has no name, that he searches the wharves looking for one. Another tale says that he only tells his victims his name before he kills them.' His mouth twitched, whimpering.

'There's something else I want to know. What has happened to the children near the docks?'

'The wharf rats? What are they to you?'

Curse the Folk and their cold views on humanity.

'I made a promise that I intend to keep.'

'Okay, okay there has been word, unconfirmed word, that there is a spirit that lurks at the wharves, a musical spirit.'

'Are you mocking me?'

'No, I swear that's what I have heard; they appear at East wharf at twilight. Maybe you'll find the girl there.'

'I didn't say that it was a girl.'

'One learns a lot when you put an ear to the wharf.'

Lydia released him as she turned, sheathing her dagger. Obake shook his head, returning his features, his eyes red rimmed.

'Lydia, this spirit isn't one to mess with.'

'I have no choice, I made a promise.'

XVII

Lydia felt a stiff sea breeze pass by her, its chilling touch cooling her agitation. She drew then sheathed her falchion; she had spent the previous hour whetting the blade.

Sobbing broke the morning quiet. The clinking of chains unnerved her. The wharf was usually deserted at this hour, the dockworkers shunning the unnerving light which brought this scene to reality.

Several indistinct figures appeared leading a trail of children chained to one another - a press gang. Lydia had nothing but scorn for them. The press gangers wore ceramic masks, their sharp features terrifying.

The dockside was slick from the waves which had passed the previous day and one of the children slipped. The captors were not kind with their charges; the child hit the dock viciously as one of the guards backhanded him. They lead the children to the end of the dock, where a man waited; she guessed that it was a man by their poise.

Lydia took advantage of their turned backs and vaulted from her hiding place. She felt the impact more than she thought she would as she rolled to her feet. The masked press gangers turned to face her at once.

It hadn't been the best idea to come alone but who could she call? The closest thing she had to friends were a faceless man, an innkeeper, and a devout member of the Orchid sect.

With sinister slowness, the gang drew long knives from their cloaks. Being a Hemlock gave her authority but no additional abilities, and she cursed herself for ever taking this badge up. The first press ganger tried to take her head off, instead slashed at her hair. You're going to pay for that, she thought; my hair is now lopsided. She buried the blade up to the hilt in the chest of her attacker, the sheer force of it jolting her arm, and then hamstrung a second who screamed, using a white gloved hand to try and stem the bleeding.

There was an audible clap and her assailants parted, their leader walked in between his assembled men.

'Impressive. I wouldn't even have thought you old enough to be a Hemlock but here I am proved wrong.'

'If you know I am a Hemlock, you know what I can do.' Bluffing, even as she knew it was it the only way she would come out of this alive.

'Precisely Hemlock, you have no abilities beyond an abundant temper.'

Blast it.

The gang master removed his mask, revealing a handsome man in his thirties with blonde curls, undercut slightly by his freckles. Something in his face rang a bell within Lydia but she didn't know why.

'Well don't make me angry then. Why do you want these children?'

'Why does it concern you, Hemlock? As far as I am aware they are human, not spirits.'

The dispassion annoyed Lydia more than anything else.

'I made a promise that I mean to keep. Release that girl, the brunette one.'

'Only the one, Hemlock? You're slipping. If I release her, will you leave me be?'

Bile rose. Lydia forced it down even as she nodded.

The gang master nodded to one of his underlings, who took a key from his belt before unlocking Madeline. He pushed her towards Lydia. Lydia had imagined Madeline to be young, no more than thirteen years old, but she was shocked to see she was no more than ten. Madeline had tears in her eyes as Lydia took her by the hand to lead her away.

'What about them? We're not going to leave them?'

'You will learn one day that the choice is between you and them, and nothing can ever be worth more than your own life.'

'But they're children.'

Lydia wished she could silence the girl. Each word made her feel guiltier. Lydia went to move away but then stopped, turning to stare at the leader.

'What is your name?'

'If I told you that I would have to kill you.'

Something wry about it made her laugh.

XII

The first drink made her dizzy but she could stand up easily enough. Innkeeper was aglow with joy with his daughter back. Lydia couldn't look at Madeline. The accusations she found there pierced deeper than the thick skin she had obtained over the years.

The common room was crowded; the spirits had found every available inn and booked every available rooms. Innkeeper, happy that his business was thriving was robustly downing ale at an alarming rate. Lydia, as little as she wanted to admit it, was happy. She was happy. She clapped along with the rest of them as the dancing started. The music was from a harper, from beyond-the-bell, her world. She hated him not for his playing but for the reminder of where she must soon return. Well that was if she lasted her twenty four hours.

'Lydia.'

Lydia started. She recognised that voice, and she still had time.

Ayaka's face wasn't angry; it was pinched at the edge as if she was trying not to laugh.

'Come to kill me, have you?' She turned from her friend, unwilling to show her face. She couldn't show her fear, her hurt.

'Lydia, you're off the hook. We have had word from Obake. That a nameless man had been seen with the twin leaf flute in tow.'

Even angry with her, Lydia could not deny Ayaka had always had the most beautiful eyes, like the first day of autumn.

'I told you but you didn't believe me. Why don't you leave?'

'Calm yourself Lydia, I only came to tell you the good news. Well that and to watch the procession. Why is it so stuffy in here? Perhaps Innkeeper needs to throw some of this lot out.'

Lydia couldn't even look at her; she had threatened to kill her and then acted as though nothing had happened. And it was stuffy; the common room was overcrowded. It wasn't usual patronage either. There were some finely woven cloaks, and meticulously stitched white gloves. White gloves! No!

The music faded as the musician motioned for a drink. The patrons that had been settled around the ledges no longer looked at her with bleary eyes. No, now she couldn't even see their eyes, their white masks sinisterly smiling in a frozen way. With deadly efficiently they flicked their wrists, revealing their knives.

Lydia glanced left to right then around; there was nowhere to escape to. Ayaka began to speak, unaware of the encircling enemies.

'Lydia you have to...' Ayaka jerked.

Lydia rushed forward to steady her. The crossbow bolt had taken her through the throat; she saw the terror in Ayaka's eyes as she tried to breathe, to keep her heart beating. Lydia caught her as she fell; she wiped the tear off Ayaka's cheek and held her close.

When Ayaka at last shuddered Lydia realised she had been gripping Ayaka's hand so tightly it had gone white.

'The price of crossing me is high, Hemlock.' The man's blonde features were bleary and Lydia rubbed her eyes. They were so sore, and dry.

She didn't look at him. 'We made a promise that I would leave you alone as long as you gave Madeline back. But you made it personal.'

Laying Ayaka softly on the ground, she brushed a hair out of Ayaka's eyes.

'I warned you that if I told you my name, I would kill you.'

'Kill me yes, but not her. You're a coward. You think by surrounding yourself with mystery you wouldn't attract the attention of the Orchid Sect. But you were wrong; Ayaka was one of their own. You had best hope I kill you before they find you. Ayaka didn't even know your name.'

'Oh she did. Glamours have the ability to make us seem that which we are not. A faceless man for example. But it's not for my safety that I hide my identity.'

The gang master nodded towards Madeline.

Lydia drew her falchion and recklessly charged. One of the masked gang members caught her outstretched hand, forcing it behind her back. Gasping Lydia dropped her sword.

'Sir...?'

'Let her go.'

He released his grip. Sensation returned to Lydia arm with painful joy.

'At least tell me this before I kill you. Why did you take the children? What good were they to you?'

'The young have the ability to see that which the adult eye cannot perceive. They can see the gaps between our world and others.'

'And if they're hurt in the process?'

'If they were hurt in the process? Do you think that I would hurt Madeline? My own niece?'

'Your niece?' Lydia couldn't connect the dots between Innkeeper and this man.

Innkeeper's paunchy form pushed through the crowd to its centre. He pulled his daughter in protectively, her head resting where his heart beat, no doubt racing.

'Brother... I thought you dead?'

The gang's leader laughed viciously.

'Dead? That is what you would rather have believed. It would make it simpler for you, wouldn't it? While you have this perfect little family I could rot in an alley.'

Lydia couldn't believe what she was hearing, that Innkeeper was this man's brother, the man who had killed her Orchid.

'Fabian, how could you do this, any of this? You were my little brother, a good boy as I remember you.'

'How could you remember? You were not there. Everything I

have now, I have had to work for. The only reason you are not dead is because I could not deprive my niece of a father.'

'Fabian, I had to leave the wharves, you and mother because...' Innkeeper used his hand as though to placate his younger brother but it wasn't working.

'You owe me a good excuse at least. Did you even know mother had died?'

'I've known for years.'

'And you didn't even attend the funeral.'

Fabian drew a knife and headed for Innkeeper. Lydia kicked his ankle out from under him and the man fell to the floor with a crunching sound.

'Enough! Stop it. Your fight is with me, not him.'

'That is where you are wrong, Hemlock. My fight will always be with him.'

'This fight is between us.'

'Have it your way. Meet me at *Bungelosenstrasse at the sixth bell.*'

Whether he thought that she was going to retaliate or not, she didn't because the only thing that mattered to her, that linked her to this world, was in this common room.

Lydia didn't realise how much time had passed. Some part of her heard a voice calling her name, somewhere in the distance.

'Lydia, get up, get up now!'

Lydia looked up to the smile. Being devoid of eyes, Obake's only tell was his voice, and his voice sounded desperate. An orchid was embroidered on the collar of his coat. He grabbed her by the collar, forcing her up, gasping as the sudden movement jerked her arm.

'I mean it, she's gone, Lydia. We need to get out of here before the orchid is burned into the door.' Obake's smile was grim. He was not a strong man but he tried with all his strength to pull her.

Another voice interrupted. 'Not the Orchid, not on my door. It's as good as a death wish.'

Lydia picked her blade off the floor, charging over to Innkeeper, held the blade at his neck. His pupils dilated. She could smell his perspiration, the fear.

He struggled for breath, spluttering.

'Let's go.'

Obake bowed before following Lydia out the door.

His egg-shaped head reflected the moonlight as she looked up to the clouds.

'Lydia, you do not have to do this. Let it go and move on. The Orchid Protocol has been renounced and you are free to leave.'

'To leave and go where, Obake? I can't return to Portsea, it's suffocating. Knowing about all of this gives me hope.'

Lydia set off for the North West District. She wanted to get away but Obake insisted on tagging along.

'You are a young woman; surely there is a trade that you can follow.'

'I am a Hemlock, bound to the Vine until it withers and dies. If I don't police the Folk, they'd tear themselves apart!'

'Not necessarily, The Orchid Protocol...'

'... led to a civil war that decimated the Folk.'

Obake nodded and then focused his attention on the path, not speaking. The uncomfortable silence fell between them and Lydia wouldn't break it.

'Lydia... I am sorry for your loss.'

Lydia kept her eyes on the path ahead.

'I know that she meant a lot to you but vengeance is not the answer.'

She turned on him. 'Vengeance is always the answer.'

Lydia pushed on ahead, until her footsteps pounded in her ears and Obake was only a figure in the distance.

<u>**III**</u>

Lydia flexed her arm, following the forms, her falchion as much a part of her as her limb. The time had been set; the place set, *Bungelosenstrasse*, and now all Lydia had to do was to survive the remainder of her twenty four hours. Obake stood at one end of the street while Fabian's men stood at the other.

Fabian stood opposite her, his blade a swirl as he approached her, curving with his body. Lydia knew him to be a good swordsman but in order to save Innkeeper's life she had to win this fight, and by the Folk she was determined. She braced herself for the first exchange, but it still left her fingers numb from the shock. Twisting, she kicked out, catching Fabian in the knee. He swore but he kept slashing. To live on the street, you had to be strong. To show weakness was to admit defeat.

Although only a girl of nineteen, Lydia had known sorrow and she had known love. And the one she loved, even though she dare not admit it to herself, had been murdered by the man before her. When she realised that Ayaka had betrayed her, that was the dagger that was lodged in her heart, but to admit weakness was defeat. And Ayaka had been her weakness.

Lydia pressed her advantage, striking until she felt the earth shift. Slipping on the sodden wood of the wharf, a jolt ran through her and she narrowly avoided a slash to her neck.

'So your brother didn't want you. Is that what this all about?'

Lydia had to get him to make a mistake, just one and she would have him.

'As if a wharf rat would understand what I have gone through.'

'Understand? That you fear to care or to trust anyone because some part of you fears they will betray you or worse that you will come to love them. That's right isn't it, that's why you hate your brother so much?'

Fabian lost his advantage, lost his mind, his skill, and Lydia took advantage. He ran straight for her, his guard open; too perfect a chance not to take. But Lydia was wary. She saw it in his eyes, the pain, and the need for an end, for release. Lydia battered away his sword and took him in the chest. A broken flute rolled onto the wharf, broken by her savage blow. It was ironic really, given the amount of trouble she had gone to get it back.

Fabian gasped as she sheathed her blade in his chest, his breath ragged.

'It hurts... so much. I never expected...'

'That is what love does to you.'

Lydia wrenched her blade up, and the cloudy relief of death blanketed his eyes. There was thud as his body fell to the ground.

Obake ran to her and took Lydia's head in his hands.

'Are you okay?'

'Get your hands off me.'

Lydia pushed him away; she turned from him and began to walk away.

'Lydia, where are you going?'

'I've had enough, I'm going home.'

'Lydia...'

'No I can't stay here, not without...'

Lydia set her path, the path that would take her directly to the Grimm Bell, take her home... back to Portsea.

The Rhythm

Charlotte Comley

Night-time windows with the lights on inside always made Jack think of the cinema. The red neon light from the open take-away sign distracted his attention from the two Formica tables with chairs attached. He opened the door of the fast food restaurant, walked to the chest high counter, and waited for the old guy to take notice of him.

'Hi, my name's Jack. I emailed. I'm researching local ghost stories' he said, stretching out a hand which the old guy ignored. 'Are you Ted?'

The man behind the counter wiped his palms on his apron and nodded.

'Did you check out our app and website?'

'No,' Ted replied. He picked up a cloth and wiped the surface of the counter.

'It's just I was told you had a story to tell?'

'Coffee?' Ted asked. He threw the rag into a stainless steel sink and got out two cardboard takeaway cups.

'Please,' Jack said.

Ted motioned for him to sit down at one of the tables.

Jack took a seat and was relieved the table was clean and dry. He pulled out a note book and black fine line pen. From the window, he could see the New Theatre Royal. Unsettled by Ted's demeanour, he was starting to regret coming here.

'Did you know the theatre is haunted by the old manager?' Jack asked.

The meeting wasn't going as planned. He tapped his foot nervously; he'd never been good with awkward silences. Perhaps it was something left from the silent years of his childhood, the endless meals when his parent glared at each other before the divorce. He glanced out at the night. A couple walked down the street holding hands. He heard a shout from someone leaving a pub but couldn't quite make out the words. It was a quiet mid-week evening. On the weekend, this street would be packed.

'Why ghosts?' Ted asked, taking the seat opposite, and putting the cups on the table. He reached into his apron pocket and put some packets of sugar on the table along with two thin wooden stirrers.

'Well, there is a little more to it than that. What I am really considering in my work is the idea of the mix of the supernatural and the urban landscape.'

Jack cut down his usual passionate speech about his academic research. This lead was a mistake, he was sure of it now. Best get it over with as soon as possible.

The old man was looking out onto the street. He cleared his throat. 'Portsmouth is the second most populated city in the England. Did you know that?'

Jack shook his head.

'And do you know how many people go missing in this city?'

'Erm not off hand, but...'

'When you pass the Big Screen and you see the faces of those who have just disappeared, do you ever wonder how? We are surrounded by CCTV cameras, we leave electronic traces, and we need a bank account to get help from the state. How can people still get lost in the city, the same way, they did in the eighteenth century?'

'What I'm actually looking for are ghost stories...'

'Ghosts?' Ted sniffed, 'They're just a shadow, an imprint, a TV rerun.' He took a sip of his coffee and nodded towards the window. 'What do you see when you look out the window? Not quite the set of a horror film is it?'

'Well, no, but...'

'Yet people still fall through the cracks. Men with jobs and wives come out for a drink and disappear. Women don't come home. The police explain it away as stress or hidden depression. And who knows how many of the vulnerable and the homeless vanish. No one even reports them.'

Jack nodded in agreement, and risked a sly look at his watch. It had been a long day at the university and he didn't feel the need to discuss the economic problems of the country. He got enough of that at work. 'There's always those who fall through the cracks in society.'

'*Falling through the cracks.* Ever wondered where that phrase came from?'

'Etymology isn't my strong point.' Jack rubbed his chin with his hand; it was more than a five o clock shadow. He would go home without a new story. Maybe have a bath before bed. He just needed to work out a way of leaving quickly and politely.

'Children know,' Ted said.

Jack gave a polite cough, "cuse me?'

'Children know not to walk on the cracks.'

Jack nodded, smiled, and took a long gulp of his coffee, pleased that he managed to empty half the cup. He put the lid on his black fine line pen and closed his note book.

'Do you see it on the pavement?'

Jack's gaze followed to where Ted was pointing. There was nothing there. Ted's pointing became more insistent. There was an empty water bottle and...

'The cracked paving stone?' he asked.

Ted nodded, stared Jack deep in his eyes and in a low voice hissed, 'Yesterday it was over there.'

Jack pressed his lips together; he was going to kill Colin tomorrow. No doubt his colleague was having a great laugh this evening, knowing that he was here with a talkative loon.

'Okay, em, if you do think of any stories, please feel free to send me an email.'

He opened his notebook again, took out his pen, and in a thin scrawl quickly wrote down the name of the website.

'I think it's a form of magic' Ted said. His voice sounded heavy, slightly slurred. 'A summoning of sorts. The salt in the air. The blood spilt from fights, the piss and vomit. Seeping down through the cracks in the pavement.'

Jack sucked in his breath and gathered up his belongings. 'Drop me a line if you think of anything' he said, getting to his feet.

Ted's hand shot out and grabbed Jack's wrist. He tried to pull his arm away and was surprised at the old man's strength. 'Can't you feel it?'

Bizarrely, Jack remembered long ago warning from his mother about men, men who liked to touch boys. He shook away the memory. This was a frail older man; he was twenty years his junior. He ran marathons for goodness sake, he wasn't in any danger. He tried to free his arm again. The old man held it fast. It felt warm, and he could feel the heat stretch up the skin above his wrist. He was about to shake the old man off when he realised he did sense something.

'Listen.' Ted urged. 'Please.'

He'd always been a sucker, Jack thought. He let himself fall back into his seat. With his other hand, he freed himself from Ted's fingers.

'Okay, okay, I'll listen.'

There was a siren, a call from a drunk. Jack shut his eyes, tried to focus.

'There's nothing, the hum of the freezers maybe?' But before Jack had finished the sentence he realised he was wrong. He wondered if it was just his own blood in his ears. No that wasn't it. It was more like a sigh. The wind then? But no, the night was still and it was too regular. There was a rise and fall to it.

'My first year of business, it was mostly just me. I had this regular customer for a time, an old boy from the city who could make a coffee last an hour or two. Told me that he thought there was a living thing under the city. I ignored him...then. But you see things in jobs like mine. On a Friday and Saturday the streets are full, gangs of lads full of excitement, women tottering on heels, and there is always a young girl sitting on a step crying. But then there is the calm. When you're cleaning up, turning off the lights and walking to the car. By the time I set up my second take-out, I began to notice patterns. Not just the weekend trade, or the fact the fights broke out on a full moon; there was a rhythm to the city.'

'A rhythm?'

Yes, the sound Jack could just hear had a rhythm. It made him remember when he'd been a child, lying on the playing field and suddenly being aware that he was a small boy, lying on the grass of a planet that was spinning around the sun and he'd been sure he could feel the world spin. Now he was a man, sitting in a burger and kebab shop, and he could feel something. But this time, it wasn't the earth spinning. He was moving, or the floor was moving, like he was on board a ship.

'It feels like we're at sea. Is there water flowing under this shop?'

'It's the city' Ted murmured.

'I can feel something under my feet like a pump.'

'No, a pulse. It's the city's pulse.'

Jack closed his eyes again. It did feel like a pulse, a regular thud. He suddenly wondered if the man was a hypnotist. Was this an elaborate joke by Colin? The city having a pulse. Nonsense.

'So you're saying that some sort of beastie lives under our feet?' Jack asked, relived that the suggestion sounded crazy.

The old man shook his head, his eyes becoming heavy. 'I've set up and run six business like this one, been working here for over forty years. There is no creature living under this city. It's the city itself that is alive. Can't you feel it?'

And Jack could feel it, he could sense the life around him.

'How?'

'I told you. The decades of blood, and salt. The deaths. I think they act as a sacrifice. I think the city is alive, and I think the city is hungry and that's what happens to the missing people.'

The door opened, and Jack jumped at the electronic beep as if startled from a dream. It was nothing more than the power of suggestion.

'You still serving mate?' the customer asked.

'Sure am' said Ted, getting out of his seat. 'Your usual?'

'Yip, extra mayo.'

'Where's your mate?' Ted asked, getting to his feet.

'Dunno. He stepped outside for a bit of fresh air didn't he, and then he didn't come back into the pub. Maybe he's pulled.' The man drew his wallet out of his back pocket. 'Can't see it though, not on a Tuesday night. And it's not like him not to text. Still I'm sure he'll turn up.'

'Hmmm,' Ted said, carving slices from the slow rotating slab of meat.

Jack picked up his pen and notebook. He smiled at Ted and left the shop. The fresh air was crisp and he was glad to be outside. He looked at the crack in the pavement and laughed. Seriously, the old guy had him going for a minute.

Walking back to his car, smiling to himself, he saw a drunk stumble out of the pub and fall to the ground. Without hesitation, Jack stepped forward to help. The inebriated guy greeted him with a toothy smile. The cut on his head wasn't deep, but it was bleeding steadily. Scalp cuts always do.

'Come on, you sit here' Jack said, pulling a hankie from his suit pocket. He tried to get the now laughing drunk to stay and offered to call an ambulance. But he laughed and got onto his knees, blood dripping on to the pavement. With a dramatic sway and a sigh that would have not been out of place in a Shakespearian production he heaved himself to his feet.

'I'm alright mate, I'm alright' he sang.

Jack watched him take a step or two, saw that he wasn't staggering quite as much, and convinced himself the drunk would find his own way home. He bent over to pick up his note book and froze.

There was a crack in the pavement where the man had bled. It looked like a large smile.

The crack had been there before, Jack thought. He scoured his memory. He'd put his notebook down. Bent down to help the drunk, handed him a handkerchief. *The crack must have been there before.*

Restless

Andrew Bailey

just the wind   the light   the items
are restless   in CEX a keyboard
shatters   flashes of light from the bed
the sound of light chains clinking   won't you
please   of children whispering   she
looked back   between the light   his legs
being lifted   her throat   from her own
hands   please won't you   secretly buried in
the wind   snatched items   still clinking
items from the wind   in the opposite direction
between the light   just restless   in the wind
between the directions   dozens of bodies
waking   dozens whispering   dozens   won't you
please   said to remain   the wind   please
why don't you   light   just

ghosting on
http://www.paranormaldatabase.com/hotspots/portsmouth.php

Killing Time

Jacqui Pack

Seeing she has twenty minutes left, Claudia puts her phone back into her bag. Still no signal. She wraps both hands around her takeaway coffee. Her stiff fingers refuse to register its warmth through the paper Caffé Nero cup. Not that anyone else appears cold, she thinks, as she eyes the man in shorts and flip-flops at the other end of the bench. The sight of his bare legs creates a rush of goose-pimples down her back. Claudia folds the sides of her cardigan across her front and reminds herself how wearing a coat would have ruined the lines of her sundress.

Jay's never been early in his life but, all the same, she can't help watching for his floppy blond hair amongst the Bank Holiday shoppers carried up from the car park beneath Central Square. A burst of drum and bass, accompanied by screams and applause drifts through from the Plaza. Claudia takes a sip of coffee as two identically dressed girls step off the escalator and hurry towards the noise. Jay sounded the same as ever when he called, she thinks, mentally replaying their short conversation. Even so, the thought of seeing him makes her empty stomach churn. She takes another mouthful and tries to convince herself that it's disappointment, not relief she feels each time a flash of fair hair turns out to belong to a stranger.

A trio of workmen in the centre of the square finish roping off a new sculpture, still hidden beneath a white canvas, just as a reporter and cameraman arrive. Claudia vaguely recognises the suited man, but she doesn't watch much local news and can't recall his name.

While she's lost in thought, a red-faced woman, an e-cigarette clamped between her lips, plonks herself in the middle of the bench, followed by a red-faced boy holding an ice-cream. Together, the pair completely fill the space Claudia had left between herself and Flip-flop Man. Fearing for her dress, she leans away from the squirming child beside her and throws a pointed look at his mother. The woman, vapour swirling from both nostrils as though she were part-dragon, blanks her and smiles down at her son, apparently seeing no problem in his handling of the dribbling cone.

It's no wonder the bloody thing's melting, Claudia thinks, as a blob of ice-cream lands by her feet. The ignorant twosome radiate heat. She shuffles to the very edge of the bench, hoping their feverishness isn't contagious. The boy kicks his legs and lolls to the side, seemingly delighted to have extra room. Claudia stands, tutting loudly, but the woman continues acting as if she wasn't there. The boy slides, almost nonchalantly, into the empty place.

Defeated by their rudeness, Claudia decides that now she's standing, she may as well kill time by seeing what's happening in the Plaza. She picks her way through the crowd, but is forced to sidestep a knot of teenagers in the narrow gap at the square's corner.

'What am I, invisible?' she mutters, venting her frustration quietly so as not to draw their attention.

An ambulance siren cuts the air. Claudia stops. Panic, rising like a lump in her throat, obstructs her breathing as the urge to run battles the fear of moving. The wailing increases then grows distant as the ambulance frees itself from the tangled traffic outside Vernon Gate. Claudia's heart bulges against her ribs, skipping and racing as though it were going to explode.

A panic attack. Just another panic attack, she tells herself, forcing her lungs to work. No different to the one on Friday night, outside Jay's. She leans against a shop window, trying to control her breathing while images, laid out like a tacky photo-story from a problem page, fill her mind. Watching the unknown woman ringing the bell; Jay's delighted smile as he opened the door; their kiss as he took the wine bottle; his hand on the woman's back as she stepped inside. In the final image, Claudia sees herself crying in the street, destroyed by her impulsive decision to surprise him. She remembers experiencing this same sensation of dying.

She covers her eyes. Jay wants to see her. Everything between them is fine. He doesn't know she was there, so there's no reason ever to mention it.

The lump in her throat begins to dissolve as her heartbeat regains its rhythm. Finding she can breathe again, Claudia lowers her hands from her face.

She gasps, unable to take in what she's seeing.

The air is thick with masonry dust. Smoke billows through the shattered glass shop-fronts on either side. Sparks and flames jump and dance within the buildings. Dismembered mannequins litter the ground. The quaint patisserie in the converted tram-shelter is no more than a burned out shell, its outside seating mangled and overturned. Claudia stares in confusion. People are strolling towards her, going in and out of the shops, oblivious to the devastation surrounding them. She blinks and suddenly finds she can see two versions of the precinct. One normal and untouched; the other a burning war zone. The two overlapping scenes flicker in and out of focus, like misaligned layers of an optical illusion that refuse to converge.

Unnerved by her bizarre double vision, Claudia hurries through the crowd and turns away from the busy Plaza, towards the waterfront. On the corner, outside the casino, she pauses and looks back. There's no sign of fire, no wreckage. The air is clean and the tables outside the patisserie are filled with customers. She bites her lip as tears film her eyes. Is it any wonder she's seeing things? She can't recall sleeping for more than a few hours during the last three nights, and hasn't been able to face eating for days, relying instead on a constant flow of coffee to keep her going. What she saw, she reasons, was some kind of daydream, prompted by the panic attack and fuelled by exhaustion and caffeine. Nothing more.

Up ahead, a cluster of gulls swoops down to squabble over a dropped bag of chips. The thin white masts of the yachts in the marina stand out against the blue sky. Claudia allows herself a tentative smile, and breathes in the sun-infused air. The overcast morning has turned into a near perfect Bank Holiday afternoon. Jay would call it a *no worries* kind of day, she thinks, checking the time again on her phone. A day when it's hard to imagine anything being or going wrong. If there was just a bit of warmth in the sun it really would be perfect.

She pauses to read the specials board outside The Old Customs House. The tables and picnic benches, either side of the entrance, are all occupied but it looks quieter inside. She wonders whether Jay might be in the mood for a pub lunch, and if suggesting one might seem pushy. The last thing she wants to do is cause a scene. Probably safer, she decides, to let him call the shots when he arrives. He might have already eaten.

Movement within the pub catches her eye. A man bursts through its doors, blood splattered across his pale t-shirt. His face and hair are daubed black with soot. A wide cut on his forehead has created a glistening red path between his eyes. A stab of déjà vu pierces Claudia as he dashes past; the conviction that she's lived this moment before roots her to the spot. The injured man runs towards the Plaza, shouting and waving his arms in distress. Claudia waits for someone to go to his aid, but no one moves. She glares at the couple, sharing a chilled bottle of prosecco, on the nearest picnic table. The woman laughs at a whispered comment from her companion and sweeps her long hair over one shoulder, revealing the brown skin under her top's thin halter neck.

Claudia's jaw tightens.

Did they not see him? Didn't they hear anything, at all?

A chocolate Labrador pokes its pink-tinged nose out from under their table, then steps out, pulling its lead taut. Its brown eyes fix on Claudia as its hackles rise, creating a ridge of disturbed fur that stretches the length of its spine. It growls, and then begins barking. The man puts down his glass to shush it, trying to hook the animal back under the table with his leg, but the dog refuses to budge or quieten. Its muzzle wrinkles as its lips lift into a snarl. Claudia backs away, wary of its sharp teeth, then hurries on towards the Marina.

The water below the yachts moored by the jetty sparkles as it catches the sun. Claudia rests her elbows on the rail above the floating walkway and looks out towards the opposite shore as a ferry, dwarfing the sail boats around it, ploughs through the harbour towards the Solent. She shivers, feeling thin, stretched out, like a ghost. Is she going mad? It certainly feels that way. Panic attacks, hallucinations, insomnia, not eating. She's making herself ill. Turning a blind eye to Jay's cheating hasn't let her un-see it. The same way that denying what she saw hasn't meant un-knowing, or un-feeling, the truth of it. The breeze plays with the edges of her cardigan, causing another rash of miserable goose-flesh to spread over her back.

Everything she felt sure of has been turned upside down, inside out. Even time doesn't pass as it should. She tries to remember leaving home, catching the bus, but the details are hazy, the memories hard to pin down. The morning feels distant, as though it happened years ago.

How long has she been wandering around Gunwharf Quays?

Long enough to feel lonely. She thinks back to the boy with the ice-cream, the jostling teenagers, the wine-drinking couple, and is struck by the irony of the dog being the only living creature to take any notice of her since she arrived.

For the first time, Claudia feels the sun's warmth on her back. After being cold for so long the powerful heat feels uncomfortable, as though she were standing too close to a bonfire. The thought leaves her imagining the crackle and hiss of flames and, for a moment, she catches a trace of burning in the air. Both hands tighten on the rail as she fights down her anxiety. No. She might be sick, she might be crazy, but she's not stupid and she won't let herself be taken in by things that aren't real. Hoping to distract herself from her mind's trickery, Claudia digs her phone from her bag and checks the time. With a jolt she sees it's already one o'clock.

She should be outside the cinema. Christ, what if Jay thinks she's stood him up?

She turns, already rehearsing an apology, then sinks to her knees. A mushroom cloud is unfolding over Central Square and a plume of acrid, black smoke hugs the legs of the Spinnaker Tower. People are screaming, running. A man jumps from the table-filled balcony of an upper floor restaurant, then another, and another. She watches in horror as they land, crumpled and broken, on top of the diners below. Fire alarms blare out from every building. People spill from doorways, dampened by sprinklers, screaming for lost children.

It's not just me, thinks Claudia, transfixed by the pandemonium. This is really happening. She laughs, ecstatic with relief, then bites her knuckles, repulsed by her selfishness. People are hurt, maybe dying.

Jay! She scrambles to her feet. Jay will have been in Central Square. Claudia pushes her way through the crowd, the only person heading into, not out of, the mayhem. Lungs filling with brick-dust, she crunches over broken glass and stumbles on displaced paving stones, carried forwards by her own momentum. People drag themselves along the ground, pleading for help; others lie motionless, silent. With the intense heat stinging her eyes and smoke blurring her vision, Claudia feels her way along the damaged shop fronts towards the square, almost tripping over a woman frantically struggling to right an overturned pushchair. She skirts around a boy clinging to the legless torso of an older man, his young face white with shock, and renews her frenzied shouting for Jay. Her heartbeat pounds in her ears, drowning out the clamouring of alarms and sirens.

Feeling sick and disorientated, Claudia enters Central Square, fighting to get her bearings amid the smoke and dust. The bench she was sitting at earlier has gone. The opening for the escalators has expanded into a crater that yawns across two thirds of the square. Car doors and wing mirrors litter the ground. A child's car seat hangs from a scorched tree. She bends, gasping for air that doesn't clog her lungs and starve her body of oxygen. Every instinct roars at her to turn around, but the thought of Jay, horribly injured, desperate for help, drives her on. She takes the deepest breath she can manage and straightens, determined to find him no matter the cost.

Her legs falter. The square is as she left it twenty minutes ago. The buildings are undamaged. There's no crater. People mill about, wandering in and out of shops as though nothing had happened. Unchecked tears run down Claudia's cheeks as the truth hits her.

Nothing has happened. There's been no explosion. No emergency.

She scans the area in front of the cinema for Jay, yearning for the familiar comfort of his arms. Why couldn't he have been on time, just once? Why arrange to meet if he can't be bothered to turn up when he should?

Claudia turns away from the cinema and, for the first time, notices the large crowd waiting for the new sculpture to be unveiled. Hope pierces her self-pity, leaving a stab of guilt in its wake. She sniffs and uses the heel of her palm to dry her tears. Jay's probably fighting his way through the throng of people right now, trying to reach her.

The television crew she saw earlier has been joined by two others. The mayor, a middle-aged woman with enough girth to display every link of her chain of office, stands on a small podium, next to a microphone. Claudia wanders along the edge of the crowd, paying scant attention to the amplified speeches, as she searches for Jay. Applause ripples around Central Square as the sculpture, a tall oval with a plaque on its front, is revealed; workmen clear away the rope barriers; the television reporters queue up to interview local dignitaries; people return to their shopping. Claudia keeps searching, unwilling to admit that she's wasting her time.

With the crowd dispersed and still no sign of Jay, she sinks, disconsolate, onto a bench close to the sculpture and tries to decide how long she should wait before giving up.

An elderly woman stops in front of the stone oval and shakes her head. 'Terrible thing,' she says to her husband. 'Doesn't feel like five years, does it?'

He mutters in agreement. 'They've done a grand job rebuilding, though. Considering how little was left.'

They linger for a few seconds, then move away. Claudia, intrigued by their conversation, wanders over to the read the plaque.

This memorial stone is dedicated to the 32 people who died on 30th May 2016, when this area was devastated by a series of bombs.

Today? She recoils, stepping backwards directly into the path of two teenage girls. Instead of stopping or dodging aside, they carry on walking without so much as a pause in their chatter. Claudia shudders as the foreign warmth of their bodies passes through her.

She stretches out her hand to the plaque, placing her fingers over the impossible inscription. The gold lettering remains visible; her skin and bones no more than shadows on the memorial's surface. She feels hollow, too drained to work through her confusion. How can today be five years ago?

Claudia's body tingles. She reaches for her bag, driven by the half-formed intention of calling her parents, but can't grasp its fastenings. Her mind races back over the things she's seen. She closes her eyes, feeling the substance of her presence fraying. Not hallucinations, she realises as the breeze plays through her thoughts, but not premonitions either. She remembers the explosions, the chaos. The pain.

She's held on, waiting for Jay for five years. But he's not coming. Not ever. It's time to forget him, Claudia thinks in her final moment of clarity. It's time for her to let go and move on.

Two Heads

William Sutton

It took so long to clear harbour customs, my daughter was
worried, but a couple of dismembered heads in your hand luggage
will raise eyebrows. Just part of the day job, transporting body parts.
Forensic Anthropologist, Esther Jardine, at your service.

'Ms Jardon, is it?' Mr Customs Man glanced from my passport to
the enormous cold box I was hefting.

'Jardine,' I told the dimwit. 'Professor Jardine.'

'Would you mind opening your box?'

The enormous cold box would admittedly be more apt for
carrying beer at the Isle of Wight Festival. 'I wouldn't mind, but you
might. Unless you're okay with dismembered heads.' Seeing his eyes
widen, I went on. 'The cold ought to knock out the maggots, but the
freezer packs may have melted on board overnight.' Amazes me how
quickly people can turn pale. They sometimes assume I'm ditzy: long
red hair, dazzling smile. What should I do? Put on camouflage?
'Don't worry. The blood's dried up. Though there will be gases. Ah,
the decay of the flesh.'

At security on the French side, they'd waved me through the
moment I mentioned the heads. But here, your average Portsmouth
jobsworth has to stick his nose into everything.

I passed him the paperwork.

He studied it for a good thirty seconds before he looked up. 'It's
in French.'

'Yes, it is. They're French heads.' I sighed. Any other country
would employ bilingual customs officers; not us. 'I'm assisting in a
French enquiry. And the French police would prefer the evidence
uncontaminated.'

'Why not send it by courier?'

'It's evidence. I have to keep it with me at all times.'

'Why not fly?'

'Le Havre to Portsmouth.' I shrugged. 'Quicker by ferry.' I've gone off flying since identifying the bodies from the Alps plane crash; but I didn't mention that. 'Besides, can you imagine getting this through airport security?'

I can examine human remains in situ, but all the yellow tape stuff I leave to the Scene of the Crime Officers. I take samples back to our Portsmouth lab: hair, tissue, bones; anything that carries genetic information. Every sample needs paperwork, but customs men will wave you through with little freezer bags. I've brought toenails, teeth, even the odd hand in a wine cooler, without raising eyebrows.

Since I moved down from the state-of-the-art lab in Dundee, our lab has become a world-leader too. Once you're known for breaking new ground in forensic anthropology, the calls never stop. We may not be Oxbridge or Harvard, but among the universities that actually do something, we have a good name. So the call from Jean Basauri of the Le Havre police was nothing unusual.

'Mum,' Lorelei called across the ferryport. Something about the place's colour scheme reminded me of my lab. Less sterile, though, and more encrusted baked beans than dried blood. We hugged. Strange: she's got over her teenage dislike of public affection, but now she's so tall, it felt like hugging a strange young woman rather than my own daughter. 'I was worried, Mum.'

I gestured to the box.

She rolled her eyes. 'Nice carry-on bag.'

I grimaced. 'Nice.' Carrion bag.

We have an agreement that I won't tell her what I'm working on if I judge it too high on the Lorelei Horror Scale. I pictured the contents momentarily: the first head quite fresh, stowed in a cool larder; the second in a more advanced state of putrefaction. They hadn't found the bodies yet – they would dig up the whole farm if they had to – but the heads were sufficient for my work. Hair and skin would tell me where they'd been for the last few months; from the teeth I'd know where their mother lived when she was pregnant. Poor desperate mothers, once we identified them through their missing daughters. This was not the news they longed for.

'You all right, Mum?'

'You've had your hair trimmed. Looks good.'

She shrugged off the compliment. Her mother's daughter. Despite her apparent disdain for appearance, she'd be dolling herself up for tomorrow's end-of-school dance – the prom they call it now, as if we were all Americans – and then a trip to France with her friends.

'My own daughter, driving.'

Lorelei grinned. 'Pick up and drop off, any time.'

'Good service.' I pursed my lips. 'And cheap.'

'You've done it for me.' She picked up the box, surprised at the heft. 'Once or twice.'

I laughed. 'Times change, eh?'

I got her to drop me at the lab. She told me I should take a break, but I had to chuck the heads in the freezer. Besides, I was dying to get to work. My task, as far as the Le Havre police were concerned, was to identify the victims. No more than that. But Basauri was no fool. This was a multiple murder. A tangle of mysteries must be unravelled.

Disappearances are typical in a seaside town, these liminal thresholds where people lose their way in life. They run away to sea; they elope, or jump overboard. It doesn't give a town a good reputation when a girl out on the town for an evening is never seen again. It's no accident that the cities with the worst reputations are always ports: Plymouth, Southampton, Portsmouth worst of all. Heaven light my guide? Heaven's light my arse. Ports have a reputation for raunchiness and recidivism. Le Havre is no different.

These crimes were only discovered because he got it wrong. A girl had got away from him. A young British lass on holiday. She ran down the farm lane, barefoot, torn clothes, bruised neck. Somehow she got to the police. She was in shock, unable to talk. They'd need to be patient: her evidence would bring a swift conviction, once we caught the bastard.

Basauri raided the farm straightaway. The perpetrator had vanished. He was in such a hurry, he left these two heads in the larder. What other horrors lurked there? The owner of the farmhouse had moved to Australia to be near his grandchildren; he'd left the house empty, letting his fields to neighbouring farmers. It was remote, far from the road, and nobody knew a thing. The perp might have squatted there for months, on and off.

Any detail I could tell him about the perp Basauri would take seriously. His crime scene crew were dusting the scene for prints, combing for hairs, fibres and suchlike. It's a male-dominated profession, crackpots raised on television shows where they decipher the scene at a glance. Continental police often go at these things like a pig at a tatty.

Forensic Anthropology, on the other hand, is 90% female. We're good at seeing the wider picture. I examined a Cornish girl's bones last year. She died tombstoning: you know, leaping off cliffs into the sea. She had weird notches on her ribs, fractures dating back intermittently for years. Of these injuries the family knew nothing. We checked the timings. You can date injuries accurately through childhood and adolescence. They coincided visits to their Irish relatives. Her uncle had been abusing her since she was tiny. That's why she leapt to her death. Not misadventure. Suicide.

I began gathering evidence from the two heads. I sent the DNA codon patterning straight through both to Basauri and our UK database. I asked for fast track processing. But everyone asks for fast track, and I don't have the clout of an investigating officer.

I got down to work. First, their hair. Head two had only clumps left; head one's was cut unusually short. I wondered if it had been cut post mortem.

Soft tissue samples – skin, eyeballs, ventricles – I prepared for mineral analysis. Blood, teeth, bone the same. The downstairs boffins would test all these in the morning. I took swabs inside the mouth. In sex crimes, the internal examinations can be pretty gruesome. With only their heads, I was spared the worst.

Something bothered me about the severed areas, but I couldn't think straight, exhausted. I went home.

Day two. To Lorelei's astonishment, before she headed off for her last ever schoolday, I actually cooked breakfast. Long day in the lab ahead of me. I should have been peer reviewing a scholarly article, but I was too curious. That sounds wrong. Most people, if they saw the things I see, bodies mutilated or burnt or chopped up, would be horrified. I tell myself: the only justice I can get for them is to find the answers. I have to be detached. To be fascinated by every detail.

Bruising on the necks, or what's left of the necks. Abrasion around the nose and mouth. Spinal columns sawn through with precision. Basauri's men should check for saws and serrated knives. It's hard work to sever a spine; this was a delicate job well done.

What puzzled, though, was how the skin around the neck had been cut. It had been cut first, before the sawing. Neat lines, even with head two's putrefied skin. A different instrument. Scissors. Sharp scissors.

I looked again. Along the neatly cut edges tiny speckles. I examined them through the microscope. I enlarged the pictures a hundredfold. Hair. Tiny traces of human hair. Not her hair. Was it his?

Basauri phoned from Le Havre. They'd found several fingerprints at the farm. No match on the French database. No previous convictions. We'd have to find him some other way.

'Esther, tell me about the victims.'

'Early twenties. Good health. Apart from being dead.' I tilted the light down toward the two heads. 'Traces of make-up. Lipstick. Mascara. Night out on the town.'

'When?'

'First head, say, three weeks ago. Second head, maybe two months.'

'Cause of death?'

'Find the bodies and I'll tell you.'

'I doubt we'll find anything. We've a hundred hectares to check. And the Atlantic Sea within five kilometres. What's your guess?'

I hesitated, looking from one head to the other. 'Strangled. Or smothered. Carefully.' I explained how the skin on the neck was so neatly cut. I told him about the abrasions, the carefully severed spine, and the hair traces I was about to examine.

'They were sedated?'

'I'd say so. Hold on.' While we were speaking, a colleague had brought in the reports from downstairs: blood tests, spectroscopy, the lot. We do use computers, but while I'm kitted up in decontamination gear, I prefer paper on my desk. 'Yep, there's a whacking load of codeine in the blood. Plus some legal high. Don't recognise it, but I'd guess MDMA family.' The oral swabs hadn't been done yet, but everything else was pretty clear. 'Mineralogy of hair and skin suggests they're from ... Bloody hell.'

'Where?'

'England. South Coast.' I was shocked the victims were so close to home. They might almost be friends of my daughters. 'I have to say, they're a dead match for Portsmouth girls.'

'*Merde.*' Jean Basauri's curse had a different motivation to mine. He was pissed off his officers had wasted all night trying to match the victims to French missing persons reports.

The investigation swung into a new phase. I'd done a cursory dental check for the French. Now I'd need the full examination pronto. Results to Hampshire Constabulary, UK Missing Persons Bureau, and to the French.

Update from Le Havre. The woman who'd been attacked had no codeine in her blood. She did have the same MDMA substitute, though she swore she'd taken nothing.

She was starting to talk. He'd picked her up in a nightclub. Others must have seen him. They were interviewing staff and clubbers; but who would remember some random guy chatting up a random tourist. She would tell more soon enough. They'd get a description, work up a photofit picture.

Basauri hoped I would find the perp's DNA on the victims. I was analysing those microscopic hair fragments, puzzled by the multiplicity of DNA, when Lorelei rang.

'You've forgotten.'

'No, no.' Check my watch. Her blasted prom. 'I'll be home any minute -'

'You're still at the lab.'

'No, I'm - '

'I'll walk.'

'In those heels? You've got to be joking.' I was stripping off the gear. 'Look, I said I'll drop you, and I'm going to drop you.'

It's good to be wrenched away from work, sometimes. Changes your thought patterns.

Lorelei got into the car, restraining herself from slamming the door. 'I'm going to be late.'

'Fashionably late. You look good.' I was biting my lip from criticising the red lipstick, the ridiculous slit in her ridiculous dress. Girls, girls. It's always the same: when they want to look like women, they end up dressing like tarts. 'That haircut, it suits you.'

Haircut. Scissors. My mind was whirring as I dropped her round the back of Gunwharf. Her friends were there in the circle beneath the lipstick tower, ready for a warm-up drink before their limo took them to some club.

'Hey,' I said as she leapt out. 'Don't I get a kiss goodbye?'

She gave me a withering look and strolled away. I watched her trying desperately not to show how flustered she felt. I wanted to tell her to stay safe, to have a good time, not to do anything I wouldn't do. You go, girl, I thought, pride welling up in me, tinged with sadness. She greeted her friends coolly; one fellow kissed her on the cheek, and off they all walked, arm in arm. My little girl, all grown up.

I was right. The fragments of hair. They were from a whole bunch of different people. Tiny strands, all sharply cut, by good scissors.

For example, a hairdresser's scissors. Then these same scissors had been used to cut the skin around their necks, so neatly, so tidily, before he sawed through their spines. It might be a ruse to confuse forensics; it might be a fetish, wielding the scissors he had used on so many people sitting in the chair trusting in the safe hands that styled their hair. I could see the headlines now: The Barber of Le Havre.

I still needed his DNA. I went downstairs to chase the oral swabs. It was late, everyone had gone, but the results were there. Someone had put them in the wrong pile.

I scanned them, my mind whizzing. The women's saliva told me nothing new, except that wasn't the only bodily fluid present. Semen, in both their mouths. The morphology of human semen is pretty clear. Both these traces were from the same man. There was a good amount of genetic coding. I sent it through to Basauri, and to the Hampshire Constabulary for good measure: might as well check the UK's massive DNA database. We can tell so much from semen – ethnicity, age more or less – but it wouldn't tell me exactly where he was from.

One more unexpected thing: a trace of hair. Pubic hair. He'd taken such care to confuse us with his scissors and all the cutting. This was careless. It wouldn't take long to find out where he was from.

Basauri phoned. The woman had talked. They were translating her evidence. He had emailed me a recording: I'd make sense of it quicker. Not allowed, for several reasons, not least contaminating my evidence. As forensic expert witness, this was information I shouldn't be privy to. Fuck protocol, though, if it helped us catch him.

I listened while I worked at the analysis. I could hear the fear in her voice as she talked about him, and the shame.

A ferry with her friends. A minibreak deal. They didn't see much of Le Havre, beyond the inside of bars and nightclubs. When this nice boy – she called him a boy, but later said he was twenty – talked about his grandad's farmhouse, where he was staying, it sounded so romantic. He'd been admiring her dancing. He kept complimenting her hair. She liked him. Felt like she'd met him before. He never said where he was from; she'd thought he was French, though he spoke English proper enough. (I paused the recording; she sounded like a Pompey girl too). They sneaked away from her friends, got touchy-feely in the corner of the club. Soon they were driving back to his place. He put on music, he stroked her hair, he made her feel good. He gave her a vodka, but she was wired already and poured it away when he wasn't looking. He was rubbing her shoulders, telling her to relax, to give in to the night. A bit of an oddball, she said. She began wondering about her friends and how she'd get back to town. They were kissing. He was rubbing her neck, her hair between his fingers, his hands delicate around her neck. It was nice at first. Then he was strangling her.

He seemed shocked when she pushed him. (No wonder: he must have put enough sedatives in the vodka to knock out a walrus.) That gave her just enough time. He chased her, but she'd been school sprint champion; even in bare feet, she outran him by a mile. By the time he'd gone back for the car, she'd escaped across the fields.

'He won't get far,' said Basauri. It was the middle of the night, but he and his team were on full alert. 'It's not like the old days when killers just vanished, leaving a trail of dead. Nowadays the trail follows them. Even a genius can't cover his traces these days. We know his modus operandi. We'll trace his history. We will find him.'

I wasn't so sure. All this evidence, and the only thing we knew was that the murderous bastard was still out there. I told Basauri my hairdresser theory.

He groaned. They'd found a bag of hair, different colours, beautifully wrapped, as if to make wigs. They'd assumed it meant more murders. Maybe it was just hair after all.

Early morning update from Hampshire Constabulary. The dental records: they'd found matches. Missing persons, both Portsmouth women. Both good-looking, both long hair. No answer from head two's family, but the family of head one had been informed. Georgia she was called. Not head one: Georgia.

Georgia had gone on holiday to France. Never been seen again. The family had provided a recent photo, though they mentioned she'd had her hair cut since. The police emailed the photo through. It was her. I told them to go back and ask where she'd had her hair cut. Portsmouth or Le Havre?

They weren't keen to disturb the bereaved family again.

'There'll be more bereaved families,' I said, 'if you don't get your heads out of your arses.'

I hated the fact that these women would be defined by their deaths. They'd be on the morning news soon enough. People would say their deaths resulted from their own folly. They'd be blamed for sexual adventurousness. Remembered because of this insane idiot who murdered them. Why couldn't they stay safe and get remembered for something else, some achievement or discovery or medical advance? God damn it, if there's one thing I must teach my daughter, it is this.

How many more had he killed? People try to understand killers, and I have tried. Sometimes I give up and say, this is inexplicable. His disrespect for humanity removes the duty to understand him. Except that he might have done it before. Might yet do it elsewhere. Only in France? How many seaside towns, how many unsuspecting girls out in clubs? What if he'd been here on the island, cutting hair?

My analysis surprised me. I pride myself on not jumping to conclusions. But I'd assumed he was French. I'd assumed he'd met these girls out there. Now everything shifted. He was English too. From Portsmouth. A hairdresser from Portsmouth.

Hampshire Constabulary phoned back. They'd got a match with the fingerprints from the farm. Barry Bolland, hairdresser, known as Bazbo. On the database, cautioned for a fight at a Fratton pub. No known address. Last workplace Hair Today, Gone Tomorrow on Albert Road. Turned out they'd sent him packing. Why? 'We employ passing talent, nothing strange about that,' they'd told the police. 'Though he was a bit weird with the customers.'

Lorelei Horror Scale 90% and rising.

He cuts a girl's hair. Perhaps she mentions she's going on a trip;

maybe he even suggests Le Havre. He happens to travel on the same ferry, he happens to go to the same club. He strikes up a conversation. Maybe she recognises him, maybe she doesn't. A little something in her drink makes her receptive to his amorous advances. They go back to the deserted farm where he has made his lovenest. He strokes their hair, rubs their shoulders, until a second pill makes them drift off to sleep. Once they are knocked out, it is time for the scissors.

A hairdresser, from Portsmouth, flitting back and forth across the Channel. He might even have been on the ferry with me, watching me heft around these two heads. He might be back in town, ready to prey on unsuspecting girls in clubs. There might be some farm over Portsdown Hill with a larder full of horror.

I thought of Lorelei. Her make-up. Her imminent trip to France. How easy it would be to make the same mistakes these women had made. A haircut. A flirtatious conversation. A few compliments. I saw in my mind's eye Lorelei greeting her friends at Gunwharf. The young man kissing her cheek rather too familiarly. Slipping his arm into hers as they walked away toward the harbourside bars of Gunwharf. An icy shiver ran through me.

Waiting at the End of the Line

Sue Evans

Today, I have returned home from London. It is mid-January, not the bright sharp sort, but the grey gusty sort that makes me uneasy. I have returned for good, although I have just one small overnight case.

I get off the train. My stop is at the end of the line – nothing but the sea from now on, grey sea with floating oil behind me, grey station platforms with discarded food-wrappers ahead of me. Most of my fellow passengers are walking in the opposite direction - pulling suitcases behind them, they troop toward the Island ferry. Some look disorientated, others are on automatic pilot. Leaving the station, I stop. Dockyard to my left, Gunwharf to my right. Gunwharf, its tower like a giant fishbone washed up from the sea and by some fluke beached in an upright position, does not tempt me at present, but when the sun shines I am sure that my mood will change. The wind is bitter and a sudden gust tosses up dust and two large takeaway cups with straws. Rubbish bins overflow with similar detritus.

The Hard is still in its slow decline before the inevitable 'regeneration'. The once-grand hotels facing the Harbour Station look bewildered and abandoned. The best they can offer at present is junk food. It is mortifying for them. Perhaps one day it will all get better.

I stop dead and my heart sinks. There he is, across the road. His hands are in his pockets, his head is down against the wind and he looks as if he has a purpose. I watch him as he passes the old hotels and turns down a narrow alley that would take him back toward

Queen Street. As he does so he looks back over his shoulder, as if he sensed something. Did he see me? Does he know me? Do I know him? I think I do and yet I am not sure. There's something on the edge of my mind and I don't want to think about it. He is of indeterminate age, my height, pale, shifty, thin, weasel-faced and underdressed against the cold. He is everything I left here to escape. He looks very familiar. I move on, but he has unsettled me, reminding me that the past can come back to me at once. The moment I step off the train, there it is, ready to catch me out as if someone let on I was coming. Of course, no-one has, nobody could, but still, he had a knowing look. Another gust of wind and I put up the collar of my dark greatcoat and wrap the thick red scarf tighter around my neck.

Better to keep walking, I feel unsafe standing still.

Of course, I came back to visit during my years of absence and whenever I visited I brought my London self and managed to leave with him just about intact. The air here still smells of oily sea, of work and ferryboats mixed with overcoats and – I think - diesel. It brings me straight back to my origins, to wet Saturday afternoons, grey Mondays, long streets of Edwardian bay-and-forecourt terraces, chewing-gum and orange street lights on wet pavements, the ordinariness of childhood here when it was a place you left if you had any claim at all on hope. The beach is itself a continuance of the pavements. In the morning sun it reveals the bits left from the night before; needles and that sort of stuff. You don't want to run your fingers through it.

Over there are the historic ships, always in the background for me, never an immediate concern. I was, I thought, an intellectual. Flags and all that military stuff were not to my taste. But the masts stayed in my consciousness and, sometimes, I would dream of being in a small boat in a harbour, at night, in black choppy waters surrounded and dwarfed by big old ships, with masts, sails, lights and flares, wondering how I got there and how I would get out.

I have no real plans for the future, no permanent home, just a flat I used to rent before I left for London. I know that I can go there temporarily while I consider my future. At present, I am feeling a little confused by the sudden change in my life. The flat is at the eastern end of Southsea sea front. I start to walk in that direction. I feel that it will do me good, clear my mind.

I pass the taxi rank. No, I won't give in and get a taxi; I don't want the taxi driver conversation. There are buses, but I don't understand the routes (only old people understand the bus routes) and I don't want to engage, to re-learn. I am not yet ready to focus, to be absorbed back into the routines. I want to walk, just walk, for now.

I walk by the subway that feeds people in and out of Gunwharf. Did they find what they were looking for today? The ones coming out have bags with designer logos so it looks as if they did. And yet they look uncertain, as if something still eludes them. Occasionally, one will stop and look back over his or her shoulder as if having left something behind.

The city has changed, is replacing its hard core with something more fetching and is trying, as I have done, to be modern. For me, it was better clothes, a better haircut, neater beard, expensive glasses, nice coat, big scarf and leather case, stuff I could barely afford but which defined the London me. The grittiness is still there, underneath. People look at me, at least I *think* they are looking at me, and I think it is because I have succeeded and I have some edge, have defeated the scruffiness of the local. Or perhaps they are just looking through me.

As I approach the railway bridge I wonder how long the London self will survive now I am here. Or will the other one return? Yes, there were always two versions of myself. One is open to possibility. That self is the one that, in adult life, I have always kept with me and so long as my energy stays up, he is there. Not bad looking, not so easy to read, shifting, keeping ahead. I have always liked to think of him as my present and my future. I don't know what he is like and neither do those I meet, and thus he always has the chance to succeed. The second version is stuck in the past. He is the self I know and others here knew, the self I was at school, in early jobs, known to my family and friends and many ex-friends. He has no authority.

A bit of a hippy. A bit of a nerd. He isn't ugly and there is nothing bad about him, but he carries the seeds of humiliation and limitation. He is my self-consciousness. If I am him, I cannot move on.

I am now at the railway bridge. Wait! Here, I am feeling something new. Or rather, something old, very old. The arches and the tattoo shop - that has always been there. I would hurry past it as a child, frightened that someone would leap out, pull me in and what? Tattoo me? I have no idea where that came from other than some confusion with a Sunday night TV Dickens serialisation working on my imagination. Imagined or real, it is something dark, something that lurks out of reach in my mind. Something I don't want to think about.

But there is also a café now, a new, chic café. I go in, get a double espresso and sit. I still feel it, the unease, a creeping sense that I should get back on the train and leave while I can. These arches have retained their atmosphere and they resent the makeover, like a tough old vagrant forced to wash, shave and wear a suit. No amount of upgrading will take away the atmosphere; it's in the walls. The woman behind the counter is looking at me as if she knows that I am different. Nobody else looks. I get up to leave.

As I leave, I see him again. There he is, across the road. He is lurking in the cobbled square, where some of the old buildings still stand. George Square. I cross the busy road and I can see him ahead, disappearing around a corner toward some more modern flats. I know he was watching me but I cannot chase him. I would not want to catch up with him and look into his face. But I carry on. I must get to my flat, get settled in and think. I cross back over the road and I head toward the Terraces and hurry down them toward the sea front.

Now I stop. There's Clarence Pier. I recall my father dismissing its garish modern frontage as 'Lego'. Even in the winter I can smell the funfair and I am in time to see the hovercraft come in and hurl stones over the gawkers. At once old-fashioned and modern, it still attracts the gawkers. I stand watching until it leaves again, rising up on its cushion of air, swinging its rear around and off. More stones, spray, squeals. I always loved it.

Grey skies, sea-spray and pebbles, I head east along the esplanade. Someone is re-painting the ornate shelters. I keep on walking toward South Parade Pier. Wait, is that him on the beach? He has his hands in his pockets and is talking to some people. Who are those people with him? They are familiar, but they don't look at me. Seeing them, I can hear something from the past, the noise of the penny arcade on the pier. Me, my cousin, my brother, with our pile of old pennies. Now the noise is gone and so has he and his companions. Strange.

Old people are bundled up on the benches with flasks. Dogs take advantage of the winter beach, dusty stones pile up by the promenade and South Parade Pier looks as if it is contemplating its narrative – the glory days, burning down, rebuilding - and now just slow, quiet, neglect. Someone is trying to swim. Across the water is the Island. Today it is indistinct, but I can just see some houses, a steeple. Suddenly I feel very, very, sad, so sad that I draw in a sharp breath and the breath seems made of air that is entirely grey. I feel as if I am made of that grey. I almost choke. It must be the cold, just the cold and the memories.

I carry on toward Canoe Lake, boats tied in the middle for the winter, rubbish floating, two swans chasing a dog, a child with a jam jar and a net. I used to do that too, didn't I?

Is *that* him, on the other side of the Lake? Is he waiting for me? I can't think why he would do that. I remember falling in there when I was nine and being pulled out by my coat. Or perhaps that was my cousin. It happened to everyone. I leave the Lake and continue on toward the flat, crossing over Eastern Parade, which hasn't changed, down a leafy side road and here I am.

The flat has changed. It looks almost derelict. The front garden has been paved over and there are weeds and bins that haven't been emptied. The flat is in the basement of a three-storey semi-detached house. I lived here for a while many years back, before I went to London. I had the use of the garden which was tended by the landlord. The flat is apparently clean and any atmosphere the building might have had has gone - chopped up, distorted, and squeezed out by the cream-painted partition walls imposed randomly over the years. There is a smell there. I don't want to speculate on its origins, but I think it is probably desperation. I lie down on the bed. I must focus my mind and decide what to do now I am back here. I am so very tired. I feel myself drifting, a sensation of falling into a deep sleep and fighting against it. As I fall, I see shadowy people around me and some of them seem to be beckoning to me but I don't want to go with them. I am not sure I like all of them. I wonder if they were always here. I do recall that when I lived here before I always felt some presence, as if something was watching, waiting for me.

I must have fallen asleep for a couple of hours. Now it is 2 a.m. the next morning. I find myself in a narrow street in the centre of town. I am sitting in the corner of a café, by the window. I know that he is somewhere around here, too. I don't remember how I got here. Have I been drinking? I awoke and left the flat late afternoon, I think. I know it was getting dark when I left. As I left the flat, I saw him over the road, heading for the Rose Gardens. I like the Rose Gardens; I have spent many hours sitting in them, wondering about the fortified walls surrounding them, looking ahead at the metal gate through which you can see the sea. It makes me think of midsummer, lazy afternoons and my mother, who knew the name of every rose. I didn't want to go there today. The roses would be grey-green stumps, neatly lined up in their beds awaiting the warmer weather and I knew that this would depress me, as it always did in winter. I also knew that he wanted me to go there and that he is up to no good.

So here I am, in the early hours, drinking coffee. I am in pursuit of something and I think I am getting closer to it, but I have lost some of my recent memory, the bit before I left London, and my mind is in a fog. I suppose I will settle down and look for a job.

Across the road from the café is just a red brick wall with small windows, part of the back of a terrace of tall buildings. It has an industrial look, the sort of permanent edifice that the Victorians built; red brick, white stone, inscriptions, embellishments. It could have been warehouses. Or it might have been offices, or something to do with the Navy. It has that look to it, the look of somewhere you might start a job at eighteen and not leave until sixty. An institution. I went away to avoid that. The building, whatever it is, does not look as if it is in use and this street is not much more than an alley at the rear of the terrace. Around to the front, on the main road, I now recall that there is just a row of shops. I am surprised that this café is still open at this time, but the city has caught up. There is clearly business in serving coffee and breakfasts to re-grouping drinkers.

There is a street lamp outside. And there he is. I didn't see him coming; he just seemed to appear from nowhere. He is wearing a duffle coat, a big scarf and a woolly hat. He has a straggly beard and he looks gaunt and cold in spite of his clothes. He seems agitated. He is standing under the lamp and he is looking away from me, across the road. He is looking at a narrow passageway between the buildings. He looks back to me, straight at me, and heads off down that passage. I take out a cigarette and light it. The café people don't seem to care. That's good.

I regret that London never worked out. I never achieved a life there, at least not the sort I'd wanted; prospects of adventure balanced with a satisfying routine of the familiar. Saturday mornings in local cafes, nights in bistros, Sunday mornings in a local pub, characters, community and the smugness of being a Londoner in one's own 'village', stuff which I suspect, without money, doesn't exist outside of fiction. It never came together. I was always vague about where I came from when asked – and I was often asked – in bars and at work. I said 'south coast'. When pressed, I bottled and said 'Brighton'. They liked that and luckily, I knew Brighton well enough to sustain the lie.

I was in London for twenty years, just surviving on low-paid artsy media jobs. Jobs I should have out-grown, projects that went nowhere, and I was stranded in bedsits at the end of tube lines in places that never felt clean and had no identity. I wasn't young when I went there, but I always thought things would get better. Then I realised they wouldn't. Down here, they thought I'd finally 'done good'. I started missing this place, a fact that confirmed to me that I had failed.

I have to follow him. I don't know why, but I think I will when I catch up with him. I leave the café and head across the road into the passageway. It is dark and I feel afraid. Walking down this passageway brings something back to me, some forgotten experience, or perhaps a dream? I seem to have trouble distinguishing dreams from reality just lately. I don't like the feeling. I don't like it because I can't remember the source of it, but I know that it is leading me somewhere bad now. I come out onto the main road, a few cars around, a couple of police officers pass by. I look across to another terrace of buildings. The old Registry, a pub now. Students are leaving, lurching, yelling at taxis. The taxi drivers look at them with contempt. I turn right and head down the Terraces toward the sea front. There is a park across the road with more University buildings. I feel excluded by that, not a part of it. I was never a part of the University thing. On this side, to my left, I can see down narrow alleys and I can feel their age, the age in the bricks. This is all University territory. And yet it isn't, it is too close to the bits they don't want visitors to see.

I feel that the borders of time and place are fragile. I look across to the jungle of high-rise council flats, a patchwork of different windows, many with their lights still on, music blaring from one, washing billowing from another, from another loud cackling laughter, and somewhere else, shouting - violence is erupting. From another flat, there is just the flickering blue light of an old TV. No. He didn't go this way, did he?

I turn and walk in the other direction, toward the city centre. It is so cold. I cross Guildhall Square. A statue of Dickens, sitting by a pile of books (presumably his own) has appeared beside the steps. I visualise large, drunken, local girls sitting on his lap. Perhaps he would have liked that.

As I carry on a crowd of loud students passes me from behind. I await a remark, but nothing comes. They overtake and lurch toward the precinct, clutching bottles and cans, hoping to catch the last hours of another club. Idiots. I walk faster. A blast of cold wind hits me as I pass under the entrance to the Square. In front of the railway station there is a queue of taxis, the disgruntled drivers honking horns at cars blocking their rank or standing on the steps of the station entrance, hunched over their takeaway coffees. I start to run. I think I see him ahead of me. There he is, head down, rushing toward the precinct. He turns right into Arundel Street.

Here it is quieter. A drunk is slumped on one of the fancy benches with the literary quotes carved into the metal backs. There are piles of discarded polystyrene burger cartons in the flower beds. There he is, ahead of me. He is standing by a parade of tired shops, outside of what I remember, almost fifty years back, as the site of the old Mecca Dance hall. This is not a literary tour; he is taking me on a tour of my youth in the city. I approach him and he turns and rushes past me.

He is off again, back up to the precinct, up to the northern end. I know where he is going. I shout to him.

'It's gone' I say. 'The Tricorn is gone.'

He glances back over his shoulder and carries on. I follow.

We are in a car park at the rear of the Cascades shopping mall. It is bleak.

He has stopped and is looking around. He looks bewildered. Then it all changes. As in a dream, the landscape has transformed. Somehow, I am not surprised by that. Why am I not surprised by that? Now there is grey concrete all around us, behind him, the entrance to a club that is no longer there. But now it *is* there, there is a light over the door. This is where I came in the 'seventies, when I still had hope.

Now he is cornered. Perhaps we have reached our final destination.

What is he saying? His mouth is moving as he rushes toward me.

Until now he has made no noise but now I hear him. It is as if the sound is being turned up on the television. He stops, he is right up close, shouting into my face.

'You shouldn't have come back. This is my city.'

His voice is young. His accent a bit Portsmouth. That surprises me; in fact, it shocks me.

'I never left it, not like you did. *You* left it. I stayed here and it isn't fair!'

He looks as if he might cry. I think what a loser he always was. He looks away and I begin to realise that I can see straight through him to the grubby wall, greasy pavement and red-lit club entrance behind. The aroma of kebabs, curry, and chips is everywhere. He looks back to me, pushes his face right into mine.

'You don't understand, do you?' he says.

I see every detail of his face. Pale skin, dark eyes fringed with long lashes, longish nose, long face, white neat teeth and full lips. Curly dark brown hair poking out from under his woolly hat, I think I feel it tickling my face. I imagine I smell his duffle coat. He is agitated, as if in withdrawal. I fear he will hit me. I know who he is. Of course I do.

I stand my ground. This concrete courtyard is a wind tunnel – it always was. An east wind is rising and lifts old chip papers and the end of his long tatty scarf. I remember that hat and I also remember that scarf because, years ago, my mother knitted it.

I know him now. He is still here and still trapped in the very walls.

At once, I remember why I have come home.

'I had to' I tell him. 'I couldn't stay in that flat in London. I couldn't stay because I no longer belonged there. I never belonged there, even after all those years.'

'They carried me out of that flat and people were staring.' (*Wait.* Why do I only remember this now?)

I think about my old flat here, the one that I have rented and was going to return to. Have I actually rented it? No. Of course not. I remember now, I remember how and why I came back down to the city and why my memory seems to come and go like a torch with a failing battery. He stands his ground, still angry, with his eyes darting side to side. I think I can smell his breath.

But now I feel relief, as if I can let go and, at once, he is not angry anymore. He has won. He relaxes, smiles, shakes his head and grabs my hand like I was his oldest friend, returned just to see him. Laughing, playful, he pulls me along with him and we pass effortlessly through that concrete wall, the wall of a club I long ago frequented. Now I see the flashing disco lights and I feel the vibration of the music and the dance floor reverberating to the stamping feet. I can smell the sweat and I am back again.

Yes, I am back for good.

Contributors

Andrew Bailey is a writer and web worker based in Sussex. His first poetry collection, *Zeal*, was published in 2012 by Enitharmon.

Karl Bell is a historian and lecturer at the University of Portsmouth, and director of the Supernatural Cities Project (www.port.ac.uk/supernaturalcities). He is the author of two books, *The Magical Imagination* and *The Legend of Spring-heeled Jack*, the latter of which won the 2013 Katharine Briggs Award. He is also an infrequent short story writer and painter. His creative work tends to focus on the monstrous, mythical, weird and darkly psychological. He has been published in the British Fantasy Society's *Dark Horizons* 53 and at everydayfiction.com/.

James Bicheno writes historical and alternative historical fiction but also dabbles in short stories in different genres, including ghost stories. He has written three novels, a novella and is now editing his latest novel. James is a graduate of the University of Portsmouth, a member of the Portsmouth Writers' Hub and the Historical Novel Society. When he isn't writing James trains for long distance runs, teaches himself how to draw and cook and may one day get round to learning how to play the guitar he bought when he was at University.

Diana Bretherick is no stranger to crime. She worked as a criminal lawyer for ten years, was a therapist with offenders at Brixton prison, London and lectured in criminology and criminal justice at the University of Portsmouth. She is now a full time writer with crime in both fact and fiction as her subject. The first in her series of historical mysteries featuring the world's first criminologist, Cesare Lombroso, *The City of Devils*, was published by Orion in 2013. Her second, *The Devil's Daughters* came out in 2015. She lives in Southsea with her husband and two small but very destructive cats.

Charlotte Comley is a writer, creative writing tutor and professional storyteller. Her fiction has been published by Ether Books, Darwin Evolutions, Flash Flood, Chuffed Books, Dagda Press and 1000 words. Her non-fiction work has appeared in magazines such as *The Green Parent, Take a Break, Woman's Weekly, The Motion Online* and *Grow It*. She has written and published ten educational resources books. She is the Celebration Editor for Words and Pictures, a SCBWI online magazine and the Editor of the Denmead Chronicle. Currently she is completely an MA in Creative Writing for Children.

Sue Evans began writing whilst acting and directing in fringe theatre. She has had work performed at the Actors' Centre, The Lilian Baylis Theatre (Sadlers Wells), and a play developed on the Soho Theatre's Writers' Programme. She also writes under her stage name: **Suzanne Bowen**. Sue has published academic articles and reviews, has had poetry long-listed for the Plough Prize, a script short-listed for the William Nicholson 'Crash Pad' competition for internet film scripts and short-listings for the *Mslexia* Short Story Prize 2012 and the Asham Short Story Prize 2013. She publishes stories on the CUTalongstory website.

Dr Alison Habens is course leader for Creative Writing at the University of Portsmouth and author of six novels, including *Dreamhouse, Lifestory* and *The True Picture*. Her key research area is the city's 'literary leyline', where 19th century writers from Kipling to Conan Doyle, H.G. Wells to Walter Besant lived and contributed to the streets' spooky atmosphere. She also runs the Ink:Well project, in creative writing for wellbeing, and teaches life-writing retreats internationally. Alison lives in an old church on the Isle of Wight and commutes to work by hovercraft.

V H Leslie is a writer, printmaker and PhD student. Her stories have appeared in a variety of magazines, journals and anthologies and her collection of short stories *Skein and Bone* was published last year by Undertow Books. She is also a Hawthornden Fellow and has recently returned from the Saari Residence in Finland where she was researching Nordic folklore. Her debut novel, *Bodies of Water* was released by Salt Publishing earlier this year. More information can be found at her website: www.vhleslie.wordpress.com

Justin MacCormack was born in Glasgow and currently lives in Portsmouth, where he studied film at university. He has been writing since childhood. His hobbies include painting little bits of plastic shaped like knights, playing board games, running the Portsmouth Guild of Role-players (blatant plug), and complaining that kids these days don't know what's what. Aside from a bunch of embarrassing erotica novels written under a pseudonym that he refuses to disclose, Justin's work has been published by Ionic Books, including his coming of age comedy "Diary of a gay teenage zombie".

Tom Millman published his first short story in 'A Blast Of The Waverley's Whistle' in The Bognor Write Club's first anthology. Tom writes fantastical tales and follows the mantra, 'Have your heart broken, heart mended, heart chilled and heart thrilled'. Tom lives in the UK, is working on his first novel, and is pursuing publishing to become an author. Tom can be contacted by email at theballadofblades@gmail.com, through his website https://theballadofblades.com/ or through his author page, https://www.facebook.com/tommillmanauthor/.

Originally from Leeds, **Nick Morrish** has worked all over the country and has now settled in Fareham. He is a fifty-something chartered engineer who does much of his writing on oil rigs and in hotel rooms. Nick is a member of Havant Writers Circle and the Portsmouth Writer's Hub. His short stories and poetry have been published in a number of magazines and he is well into his third yet-to-be-published novel. *Still Dark Water* is fairly typical of his attempts to inject a little mystery and magic into the mundane modern world.

Jacqui Pack writes both fiction and poetry, and holds an MA in Creative Writing (Distinction). She was awarded *Long Story Short's* 'Story of the Year 2009', was among the winners of *The London Magazine*'s 'Southern Universities Short Story Competition' and, in 2016, received shortlistings at both the Worthing WOW and Winchester Writers' Festivals. Her work has featured in a variety of publications including *Litro Online, Swarm, Synaesthesia, Storgy*, and *FlashFlood*. Further information can be found at http://jacquipack.jimdo.com or via @JPCertHum.

Matt Parsons is an artist and writer. His video work often involves narrative and text. Since completing an MA in Fine Art at Goldsmiths, he has exhibited internationally and collaborated with other writers and poets. Matt is currently working on an anthology of short stories of the weird and uncanny.

Joseph Pierce is a 22-year-old student living in Southsea. He is currently working towards an MRes in History at the University of Portsmouth, much of which provides inspiration for his writing. The bulk majority of his writing takes place in 19th and 20th century settings, and he hopes to publish one of his novels in e-book form within the next year.

Stephen Pryde-Jarman is the author of the alternate history thriller *Rubble Girl* (Five stars on Amazon) and the upcoming comedy *John, Paul, George, Flamingo*. His film adaptation of *Pride and Prejudice* was sold to a German Film Company and his screenplay about a Gay footballer was taken to the Cannes Film Festival. His collection of comic short stories *The Resurrection of Thomas Zoot* has just been released in Japan and Germany and is also available on Amazon.

Roz Ryszka-Onions was born in Manchester, obtained a B.A. in German and Politics from Salford University and then moved to London to work in media sales. Roz has since worked as a clairvoyant medium and has had numerous features published in the glossy esoteric press about angels, crystals and time. She now lives with her husband and daughter in Warblington and writes full time. Her novels include a volume of ghost/mystery stories *Jagged Shadows*, supernatural thriller *Hidden Evil*, psychological thriller *Deceit in May* and a story of revenge from beyond the grave *When Love Dies*.

Helen Salsbury is a novelist, short story writer and yoga teacher. Her writing explores the complexity of relationships, and how the environments we live in shape us. She is an avid reader and student of human nature whose work reflects her interests in history, art, literature and philosophy. She inherited her love of nature, which is central to her writing, from her mountain-climbing father. She is currently working on final edits for her debut novel *The Worry Bottles*. Read more at www.helensalsbury.com.

Susan Shipp is a writer. She holds an MA in Creative Writing (Distinction) from the University of Portsmouth. In 2014 she was among the winners of *The London Magazine's* Southern Universities Short Story Competition. Her fiction has been featured in *Flash: The International Short-Story Magazine*, *FlashFlood*, and *The Elizabethan Noyses of Wymering Manor'* part of the Much-Ado-About-Portsmouth Festival in 2016. She is currently involved in a writing collaboration for Voices at the Kings Theatre, and the completion of an historical novel.

William Sutton teaches Latin and Greek, bats aggressively for The Authors CC, and plays in chansonnier Philip Jeays' band. He has written for *The Times*, acted in the longest play in the world, and played cricket for Brazil. His novels pitch Sergeant Campbell Lawless into 1860s London, a city of riches and poverty, literature, loneliness, crime, fraud and road works at King's Cross — unimaginably different from today. As he unearths the dirt beneath the cobblestones, Lawless becomes familiar with the bowels and sinews of the Victorian metropolis.

Rebecca Swarbrick has been writing poetry since she was able to write, beginning with the epic *Rabbit Feet* and continuing to be influenced by the absurd; in poetry that is at its best accompanied by silly costumes and Dada-style backdrops. Her most recent inspirations include: clouds that look like broccoli, moths that don't like the light and her little son David. She is currently in the process of writing a novel that she hopes to one day complete.

Lightning Source UK Ltd.
Milton Keynes UK
UKOW06f1507241116

288453UK00001B/61/P

9 780995 639409